I0599091

THE ART OF SCRYING

MYSTIC'S END MYSTERIES BOOK 4

LEANNE LEEDS

BADCHEN PUBLISHING

The Art of Scrying
Published by Badchen Publishing
14125 W State Highway 29
Suite B-203 119
Liberty Hill, TX 78642 USA

Copyright © 2020 by Leanne Leeds

All rights reserved.

No part of this book may be reproduced in any form or by any electronic or mechanical means, including information storage and retrieval systems, without written permission from the author, except for the use of brief quotations in a book review.

For permissions contact: info@badchenpublishing.com

THE ART OF SCRYING

ONE

"But I *know* how to scry," I told Miss Bessie as we gazed at the open magic book. "When I was a fortune teller, scrying was *literally* what I did for people. It's not something I need to *learn* to do."

"Well, clearly, the book disagrees with you, dear," Miss Bessie said as her bony finger tapped the page scrawled with scratchy writing. "There are a hundred blank pages of parchment in this book and only one with a message. The message is clear as a bell to me." The old woman squinted up at me. "You *really* want to argue?"

"You know, I seem to recall something like this in one of the *Harry Potter* stories," I said as I closed it. "Paper that had messages spontaneously appear on the paper in a book or something. It didn't work out well for him."

"You're *not* Happy Potter, dear," Miss Bessie said, patting me on the arm.

"*Harry* Potter," I corrected.

"Her, either."

"He's a...oh, never mind," I said as I slipped the book beneath the counter. "I'd feel a lot better about this book if I knew where this information was coming from."

"You'd know a lot more about where this information was coming from if you would sit down and let me tell you more about where *you* come from," Miss Bessie pointed out while shuffling over to get herself a cup of coffee. "You are the descendant of a proud tradition in this town. A proud tradition that you are *refusing* to learn anything about."

"And I've explained why that is," I told her for the hundredth time. "Look, I've agreed to work with you on this book, on the mystic thing," I said as I turned and looked her in the eye. "Who I am, why I was abandoned as a baby? That's *intensely* personal."

"At least let me explain to you about Mary—"

I held up my hand to silence her before she could tell me anything more about Gabe's mother.

"But Fortuna—"

"You told me that book's purpose was to tell me anything I needed to know. *Anything*. Anything I *needed* to know. Correct?"

Miss Bessie frowned. "Yes, that's what I said."

"You've told me I need to be careful in this town because there are some people *against* magic," I said, holding a finger up. "You told me that I need to work with you so that *the book* can tell me what it wants me to know," I added, holding a second finger up. "And you told me how fast I go, how far I dive in, is up to *me*." I waved the three digits at her. "Anything incorrect about what I just said?"

"No, but—"

"No buts," I cut her off again. "I've made my decision. I want to discover things on my own, learn things on my own. I watched my friend Charlotte get bossed around by history and her ancestors like she was low man on the totem pole. I don't want to make decisions about people, or this town, based on the past."

"You know you're driving her *crazy*, don't you?" Spike, my ghostly roommate, said as he floated around my art shop. Gideon, my greyhound, chased him excitedly. "You have self-discipline I wouldn't have. I can't believe *your* curiosity isn't driving *you* crazy."

Gideon sent images of me, again, looking away

and holding up my hands as if I was pushing against an invisible wall.

"Thanks for your input, you two," I told them.

Miss Bessie put her hands on her hips and narrowed her eyes at me. "You know, there's a reason the book won't open unless the both of us are here. Even a dead man and a dog know that you *should*—"

Miss Bessie was interrupted by her caretaker, Claire, snoring from the sitting area in the front of my gallery.

"I wish that girl would just let me come here on my own," Miss Bessie complained. Claire rolled over and drooled on my couch. "I feel bad having to put her to sleep, but I feel even worse that she's drowning your couch in saliva."

"Why don't you just tell her about your magic? She knows about mine." I shrugged.

"The whole town knows about *yours*, Miss Show-It-All," Miss Bessie snapped. "Lulu and Emily have told everyone about your little boarding of Tom the Terrible after he croaked."

"I'm not going to get into an argument about that again," I told the old woman. "It hasn't been that much of a hassle."

"Oh, no?" Miss Bessie pointed to a hopeful face peeking in through the storefront window, a five-dollar bill clutched in her hand. "That's not even a local. They're coming from out of *town* now."

* * *

M iss Bessie wasn't wrong.
I moved to Mystic's End, intending to get to know the small Arkansas town I had been discovered in. Me. A foundling on the courthouse steps, adopted to a wealthy California family I never felt I belonged in.

And as my greyhound Gideon was fond of reminding me, I've turned *away* from that information every chance I got.

"Do you think you're ever going to let Miss Bessie tell you about the mystic thing?" Spike, my spectral roommate, asked after Claire and Miss Bessie left to head back to Mystic Memories, the old folks' home that the mature women lived at.

"A couple of months ago, I would have said yes," I answered as I cleaned up the counter to get ready to open my art studio. "Now, I honestly don't know. I don't want to find out a bunch of things and then feel some sort of obligation from that."

Spike frowned. "What do you mean?"

"My friend Charlotte became the ringmaster of a magical circus, right?" I told him as I straightened up the canvases. "At first, she just thought it was her job to keep the circus running. You know, mend tents, balance the books, heal people. Just normal boss of circus stuff, right?"

"You've told me some of the stories from the Magical Midway," Spike said leaning toward me. "That's *not* what wound up happening."

"Nope, it's not."

"But if she hadn't known all of that stuff, it still would have *happened*, right?" Spike pointed out. "Not knowing the history wouldn't have changed anything."

"Maybe not. But maybe it would have made her decisions in the moment easier to make. Each time a situation occurred, she had to take into consideration the history that *created* the situation, what her *uncle* wanted her to do, what her *father* thought she should do, what impact it would have on—"

"Wait a minute," Spike interrupted. "It sounds like you're advocating for a position of ignorance being bliss or something. You think a good leader should ignore history?"

"Aha, there it is." I pointed to him and raised my eyebrow. "I'm *not* a leader. I never *agreed* to be *the* mystic of Mystic's End. That ornery old woman just slapped me and said I was."

"But...but now you *are*. So, shouldn't you figure out what that entails?"

"I will, in my own way, and in my own time," I told him. "No one's going to dictate who I am to me anymore. Charlotte gave me a choice to become a full-fledged witch. I want that same choice here."

An image of me, hiding in bed, holding a pillow over my head, was thrust in my mind. I glared at Gideon. He barked.

"Good luck with *that*, I guess," Spike informed me while floating toward the stairs. "I'm with Gideon," he said over his shoulder. "I think it's a stupid decision. You're *already* the mystic. And you didn't have a choice. Maybe you should find out what it entails instead of just refusing to look into it."

"Says the ghost that was trapped in a building for twenty years by himself because he couldn't bother to figure out how to open a door."

"Says the ghost that would have given *anything* for someone to walk through *that* door to explain what was happening to him at *any* point during those twenty years." Spike turned and looked at me. "Look, I can kinda see what you're saying, Fortuna, but I agree with the greyhound. I think you're just avoiding the inevitable. The key word being *avoiding*."

"Thank you both for your opinions," I said harshly.

"Hey, we're *just* trying to help." Spike's

expression grew concerned.

"Appreciate it. Don't need it," I told him and turned away to open up my art studio, the Mystic Moon Gallery.

* * *

"So you *don't* think he's cheating on me?" the woman asked me, her eyes hopeful.

"I didn't *say* that. I said that I think you have to examine *why* you're in a relationship where you don't trust your partner," I said, sighing with exasperation. "I can't tell you whether he is or he isn't."

"You mean you *won't*," the woman spat at me. "What kind of a psychic are you, anyway?" she said throwing the five-dollar bill down on the counter. The woman then turned abruptly and stormed out.

"This is an art gallery, not a tent at the circus, ma'am!" I called out after the woman was well away from the front door and halfway down the street. I rang up the five-dollar reading and contemplated raising the price. Or, well, *setting* a price—once word got around that I would do readings, I did them for donations only. The money raised would be donated to the Mystic's End Greyhound Rescue, a non-profit organization the helped the retired racers find homes.

"Bad day?" Pepper asked, walking into the shop.

"Maybe letting it get around that I would do readings *wasn't* the best idea I ever had," I told her, and then shared the results of the reading. "People don't come to hear they need to work on something. People come for easy answers and confirmation. They hear what they *want* to hear."

"*Was* her boyfriend cheating on her?" Pepper inquired.

"Well, yes, but that's not the point. I can't tell someone something like that." I shook my head.

"Why not?" Pepper asked. "*You* know. *She* suspects. *He's* a liar. Why not just confirm it and let her get on with her life?"

"People have to make their own mistakes. If you help them cheat their own discovery, they'll never learn," I said.

"Boy, you *really* can't decide which way to go, can you?" Pepper asked while pulling out a bag of chips. "On the one hand, you're all *I am magic, see me fidget-finger,*" she said, crunching the chips loudly. "On the other, you're like *you have to learn your lesson on your own.*"

"The two things are totally different," I argued.

"Yeah, sure, whatever." Pepper laughed and held out the bag of chips. "You were magic-ing all over the place with the dead guy in the rock, and now you won't tell a tourist her boyfriend's cheating on her. You have a weird sense of when it's appropriate to cheat."

"This coming from the journalist that regularly breaks into the police file cage to get the information she's not supposed to have," I pointed out.

Pepper's face crumpled and tears welled up in her eyes. I felt like an absolute jerk.

"Jeez, Pepper, it was just...I didn't mean..." At the sight of my stammering, she threw her head back and laughed with delight.

"You're a terrible person," I told her.

"You know, for some reason," she said, still chuckling as she picked up her bag of chips. "When I pull the wool over *your* eyes? It makes me feel *so* much more accomplished. Some psychic you are," she added, still snickering. "Chip?" she asked, holding out the bag.

"Is this *beat up on Fortuna* day?"

"It's too much fun; it can't be relegated to just one day," Pepper said, smiling warmly at me. "You know, you *should* take it as a compliment. A couple of months ago, I was too afraid of you to tease you like this."

"Let's go back to that," I suggested.

"Naw, I like it better this way," she said, balling up the empty bag. With a quick toss, Pepper sent it sailing toward the trash and then looked around. "Where's Gideon?"

"Upstairs sleeping, I think."

"Mind if I take him with me to the park?"

"You want to take my dog to the park?" I asked curiously. Well, more like suspiciously. This was Pepper, after all. "*Why* would you want to take my dog to the park?"

"I just do."

"You never want to *just do* anything. Spill it," I told her. "Otherwise, the answer's no. I don't want Gideon to get hurt."

"Oh, fine." She rolled her eyes. "Ollie takes a walk in the park every day at lunch," she said, her eyes casting away from me. "I just wanted to go meet him there without—"

"Looking like you were going there to meet him? This sounds suspiciously like you're investigating Ollie, or you're trying to go out with him." My head snapped up as I stared at her, my eyes narrowing. "Are you investigating *Ollie Kane?*" I asked, aghast at the concept.

"No! No, I'm not *investigating* him," Pepper assured me.

"Then...wait...I'm so confused," I told her as I passed my hand over my eyes. "I thought you and Gabe—"

"Me and Gabe went on a date last night,"

Pepper stated.

"Wow," I said after a few moments of shock. I was seriously impressed that both of them had kept that hidden from me. "And?"

"He's my best friend. Well, along with you." she smiled. "And I love him, I *really* do. But...we're just not...there's love, but it's not *that* kind of love anymore. Not for either of us," Pepper said slowly, pausing more times than I thought Pepper was capable of. My eyebrow rose. "What?"

"I didn't even know you guys were going out on a date."

"We didn't want to tell anyone," she explained. "We did have a long talk, though, and Gabe mentioned that Ollie's been talking about me a lot lately."

"*Ollie Kane?*" I asked, trying to picture the spitfire blonde reporter and the long-haired, friendly biker together. "You don't think it would be awkward, dating Gabe's *best friend?*"

"Why would it be?" she asked, her eyebrow raised. "So, can I take him?"

"Who?" I asked her, my head spinning.

"Gideon?"

As if the greyhound heard our conversation, he scrambled down the stairs, leash in his mouth. He skidded to a stop next to Pepper and wagged his tail.

TWO

It was quiet in the shop as I sat and ate my sandwich. With Gideon out in the park and Spike visiting Liz next door at her salon, I sat on my stool at the counter and enjoyed the quiet.

It was a quiet I *rarely* had.

I contemplated everything that happened since I moved to Mystic's End. The end result was the realization that I came all the way out here without really having a plan.

Oh, I *thought* I had a plan.

Move to Mystic's End.

Don't tell anyone I was a witch.

Investigate the history of the town, hoping I could discover who my birth parents were. Why I had been abandoned. Why I had been born with some psychic ability, a supernatural ability that made me *miserable* growing up as a child. But a skill that, less than a year ago, required my friend Charlotte to transform me into a real witch.

Point of fact? I did none of that.

Had the town been some boring small town in Arkansas, *maybe* I would have. But one catastrophe after another—admittedly, more minor disasters than I had been used to at the Magical Midway— seem to pull my attention from my own story.

A slap from Bessie Baker had changed everything.

Well, kind of.

Okay, it really hadn't changed *much* of anything.

Because I was determined not to let it.

I sighed and threw my paper plate in the trash.

Was Gideon right? Was my determination not to delve too deeply into the history of this town to understand what the Mystic's End mystic was...was I just refusing to face reality?

No, I told myself.

I was practicing self-determination. Something I watched my friend Charlotte *struggle* to do. The moment she asked questions, she was subject to powers and influences she hadn't realized her inquiry would call up.

I was being...practical.

Pragmatic.

I mean, I always *was* a psychic, that wasn't anything new that happened to me when I walked into this little town. I had never been dishonest about it with the people of Mystic's End—*everyone* knew where I came from.

Especially in this gossip-stricken nest of nosy busybodies.

Being open about what I could do—okay, *some* of what I could do—wasn't really dissimilar, didn't make me any different than who I was when I moved in.

* * *

"Fortuna!" someone spoke sharply.

My eyes focused, and I saw Gabe Wilcox standing in front of me.

"Hey," I said as I shook my head. "Sorry, I was just thinking. More deeply than I thought, I guess. How's it going?"

Gabe nodded. "Everything okay?"

"Yeah, I'm just—hey, why didn't you tell me that you and Pepper were going out on a date! It sounds like the two of you getting back together happened—and then ended—before I even knew what was going on." I crossed my arms and raised one eyebrow.

"We've been meeting privately for a few weeks without telling anyone." Gabe shrugged. "The whole thing with Tom Wilson and the fight we all had...I don't know, Fortuna. It brought up a lot of emotions in both of us, and I think we wanted to figure out what those were once and for all."

"And what did you figure out?"

"Pepper is one of my closest, dearest friends, and I'm one of hers. But any *attraction* we have for each other is just that. A deeply affectionate friendship born out of years of history." Gabe looked down for a moment and then met my eyes. "Did you know she was the first person I talked to about my mother's death?"

"No, I didn't know that."

"She was." Gabe nodded. "I can't even remember my life without Pepper in it. But we realized our relationship, unique as it is, isn't really *amorous* anymore. I think the pain of being apart, of being angry with each other, my being worried about her—it seemed like it *could* be romantic."

"How did you figure out it wasn't?" I asked him, curious.

"We kissed last night." Gabe flushed pink, and then rolled his eyes. "Or, well, we *tried* to. That attempt made crystal clear our relationship is definitely *not* sexual."

"So, you decided to foist her on Ollie?"

Gabe laughed. "Ollie and Pepper are two of my best friends. They've known each other for years, too, but I was kind of the link between them, you know? I noticed during the rock thing that...Well, let's just say I think there *might* be a spark there."

"You're as much of a matchmaker as your grandmother."

"Is she still harping on you to marry me?" Gabe chuckled. He held out his hand. "Well, I'm available now, you know."

"Gabe, you were available *before*," I pointed out.

Gabe nodded and dropped his hand. "I was, but it looks like Martin Salvi got there a bit faster than I did."

"Got where?"

"To you," Gabe said. He turned around and stared absently at a painting on the wall. "Maybe I should go ask Evangeline Laroux out on a date. I could give you and Martin a break from her incessant need to try and land him."

"Martin and I are *not* dating."

"Does *he* know that?"

"Since we don't actually go out anywhere, I *assume* so."

Martin Salvi, the operations manager of the Mystic's End Entertainment Complex, was handsome, rich, and *cagey*. As the son of one of the most famous mafia dons in the country, I supposed *cagey* was an inherited personality trait.

Then again, this *was* Mystic's End.

Almost *everybody* was evasive at some level.

"It seems like he's over here quite often."

"Detective, have you been spying on me?"

"I do drive around the town, you know." Gabe turned and smiled. "It's part of that whole detective thing, looking for crimes. Your shop is in the center of town."

"He parks in the back," I pointed out.

"Jeeves stands out front." Gabe pointed toward the front door. "It's kind of hard not to notice a security guard standing in front of an art gallery in the town square."

"Okay, okay, I get it. Everyone knows my business. It's not exactly news that everyone in this town is up everyone else's butt. Now that we finished with the requisite round of romantic teasing, what are you stopping by for? Just bored?"

"Actually, I had a question for you," Gabe said as he leaned forward. "I noticed that my grandmother is spending an awful lot of time with you. Which, you know, could be great if you're helping her get into more art." Gabe walked closer to the counter and leaned on it. "Thing is? I don't see any art in her room. Or by her on these walls," he noted, thrusting his chin toward the wall. "So, I have to ask—*what* are you and my grandmother doing every day?"

Examining a magic book, Gabe. Because your grandmother was a magic mystic person for years and you had no idea.

And you have no idea that the earth upchucked a magic book for me.

Or that your grandmother has to be here for me to open it.

None of which I could say because Miss Bessie had kept everything magical from Gabe for his *entire* life. I was the first paranormal he'd ever met.

Well, that he *knew* of.

"Have you asked *her* what we're doing?" I answered his question with a question.

"I have," he said.

I waited.

He stared.

"And what did she say?"

"Well, how about *you* tell me what the two of you are doing first," Gabe said, smiling widely. He was making no secret that he was enjoying my discomfort. "Then we can compare notes, see if the answers match."

"You're interrogating me," I accused him.

"If I was interrogating you, I'd be *much* less charming," Gabe said. Then he winked.

"Am I interrupting?" Martin asked, advancing

into the store toward Gabe and me, his expression blank. I could sense the jealousy in the air as he took in Gabe's closeness to me. If the envy energy had been paint, my walls would have been bathed in green.

"Aren't you always?" Gabe asked him flatly.

Whatever friendship or bond or unity I had perceived a couple of months ago between Gabe and Martin was no longer present in their relationship. The low hum of antagonism buzzed around them both.

"Shouldn't you be working?" Martin asked Gabe pleasantly. Without pausing a step, he walked behind the counter and stood next to me. It was an act of casual one-upmanship that made Gabe bristle. I stared at Martin with a raised eyebrow, and he winked at me—confirming that was his intent.

"Shouldn't *you* be?" Gabe countered without answering.

"That's one of the benefits of being the boss, Wilcox." Martin smiled. "Whatever I decide to do is working because there's no one to tell me it isn't." Turning to me, he held up a bag. "I brought Gideon bacon. Where is he?"

"At the park with Pepper."

"Pepper?" Martin asked, surprised. "Why is he out with her?"

"Why not?" Gabe asked him.

"Apparently, Pepper has a little crush on Ollie, and she borrowed Gideon so she would have an excuse to be in the park at lunch." I watched Gabe frown as I mentioned Pepper's interest in his biker friend. For a moment, I thought it was because he wasn't quite as over her as he claimed.

"I thought *you* and Pepper were together?" Martin asked Gabe.

"That was a long time ago."

Martin looked Gabe up and down, and then glanced over at me. Gabe's gaze remained steady. You *might* even say it was a little amused.

That's when I realized he didn't want *Martin* to know he was a threat again. Before either of them could say anything else, the chimes on the door rang out. Azalea Cotton walked in to work the afternoon shift of her high school work-study program.

"Game on, then," Martin murmured quietly.

Gabe chuckled.

I blushed hotly and rolled my eyes.

* * *

"You are an *awesome* friend," Pepper said as Gideon pulled her across the painted concrete floor. "I don't think Ollie suspected a thing when we casually, *accidentally* met along the bike path he walks on every single day." As Pepper leaned down to unclasp Gideon's leash, his nose jerked up into the air and twitched.

The dog shoved an image of bacon into my mind. Mountains of bacon surrounding him. So much bacon. Bacon, in every direction.

"I thought you were a *sight* hound. Yes, Martin brought you bacon, dog." Reaching under the counter, I held up the bag and shook it. "Azalea, can you handle the front for a bit? I don't want Gideon to get bacon bits all over the shop."

As Azalea nodded, Gideon looked offended at the idea so much as a bit of bacon dust could escape his mouth.

"You move fast," I told Pepper as we walked up the stairs. "Kissing Gabe last night and stalking Ollie today?"

"Oh, you heard about that, huh?"

"Gabe stopped by while you were out."

"I wouldn't say it was a kiss so much as it was a vertical game of Twister played with magnets in our mouths polarized to repel at all costs," Pepper called gaily from behind me. "Gabe and I are north and south ends pulling toward one another, to a point. We found the point where the poles flip last night."

"And that point is?"

"Anything romantic." Pepper grinned, plopping down on a stool and leaning on the counter. "Frankly, it was good to know for sure. That thing when he landed on top of me, and I got all hot and bothered? Turns out I just *really* like that cologne." Sitting down, she grabbed a piece of bacon off the plate I prepared for Gideon and took a bite.

"You realize that bacon is for the dog, right?"

"Bacon is bacon, and if Martin brought it, it's fancy bacon from one of the fancy restaurants over there at the Complex." Pepper grabbed another slice as a low growl emanated from the drooling greyhound. An image of me hitting Pepper on the head with a stick was thrust roughly into my mind.

"Be nice," I warned him.

The growl turned abruptly into a whine.

"Hey, speaking of the Complex, feel like getting dolled up and going out to dinner tonight?" she asked. "We've been staring at that book for a solid month."

"Are you asking me out on a date?"

"Ha ha."

I thought about all the things I had been planning on doing that night. Rearranging the paintbrushes. A shipment of new paints just arrived and I wanted to try them out. Then I shrugged. "Sounds like fun, actually."

"Want to ask Liz and Claire?"

"I'll text them," I said, reaching for my phone.

A night out with the girls sounded fun.

THREE

"Why can't *I* have a night with the girls?" Miss Bessie asked sharply as we helped her slide into one of the large circled booths overlooking the greyhound track at the Centre Club. "*I'm* a girl. Didn't even *think* to invite me? Well, lucky for you, I don't *need* an invitation. I'm too old to wait for one of those, thank you very much."

With Miss Bessie ensconced on the aisle seat, the four of us crossed to the other side of the table and lined up to slide *all the way* around the u-shaped cushioned bench. "Oh, no," Liz said pointing at Claire. "You are absolutely going in first."

Tomboyish Claire sighed and clambered all the

way around the large table. She was followed by Liz, and then Pepper, and then me.

"We're happy you're here, Miss Bessie," I told the old woman.

"Please," she scoffed. "You'll have to learn to lie better than that if you want to make it in this town as an out witch, Fortuna."

"Miss, that was a little rude," Claire said in a low voice. "It's not nice to call people names."

"I didn't call her a name! She *is* a witch!"

This would be a fun dinner.

Claire tried to correct the old woman again. "Miss Bessie—"

"Speaking of an unexplainable phenomenon, why on earth are the two of you both single?" Miss Bessie gestured toward Liz and Claire with her water glass. "You're both cute, you're both lesbians. Why have you two not got together yet?"

"Are you saying that the two of us should date each other just because we're both gay?" Liz asked in disbelief. She glanced at Claire, but Miss Bessie's assistant just shook her head in defeat.

"Well, you *could* date Pepper here, but since she's straight as an arrow, I feel like that wouldn't work out so well," she said, pointing at Pepper.

"I wouldn't say I'm straight as an *arrow*," Pepper told Miss Bessie. "But yeah, I admit there

are certain body parts I have a great affection for."
Pepper smiled widely and grabbed her water.

"You can *buy* those, you know," Liz told her,
snickering. Claire blushed.

"Settle down, you might make Fortuna's head
explode," Pepper joked while pointing to the hot
pink staining my face.

"Ladies." A handsome waiter appeared out of
nowhere and stood in front of us. "Welcome to the
Centre Supper Club. My name is Chris, and I'll be
your waiter this evening. Mr. Martin Salvi wished
me to convey his *delight* that you've come to visit us.
He wishes me to inform you that this dinner has
been taken care of. Please order whatever you wish,
and we will be honored to serve you." The
handsome, dark-haired waiter bowed ceremoniously.

"How does he *do* that?" I asked no one in
particular. "I didn't even tell him I would be here
tonight."

"Who cares?" Liz said eagerly plucking each
menu from our hands. "In that case, Chris, we're
going to have the nine-course menu dégustation,
with the wine pairing option."

"Nine courses?" Pepper asked, shocked.

I looked at Liz. "What on earth is that?"

"The Chef's tasting menu," Liz told me
enthusiastically as Chris accepted the menus and

bowed again before disappearing. "It's two-hundred-and-twenty-five per person. I've *always* wanted to try it, but it's so pricey I just never have."

"*Dollars?* Two-hundred-and-twenty-five dollars per *person?*" I asked, horrified. I was raised pretty well-to-do, but I couldn't ever remember sitting down for dinner with a price tag *this* high. Claire sat with her jaw dropped, staring at Liz.

"Yup." She nodded, smiling. "And double *that* for the wine pairing."

"Did you just order us a twenty-five-hundred dollar dinner to take advantage of the fact that Martin Salvi is trying to get in good with Fortuna again?" Miss Bessie asked Liz incredulously.

"I did." She grinned. "You bet."

"Good girl." Miss Bessie nodded with approval.

"Seize the day, that's what I say," Pepper agreed.

Chris appeared in front of us once again, clapped twice, and a swarm of waiters placed large plates with a paltry quantity of meticulously arranged food in front of us. "Glazed Oysters with Zucchini Pearls and Ossetra Caviar," he told us, opening his arms wide as if he was announcing a famous opera singer.

"We're *starting* with caviar," Liz said excitedly.

"And not just any caviar," I said, staring at the

golden-yellow eggs. "That's the second most expensive caviar in the world."

"Mr. Salvi sends his apologies that the Centre was out of Beluga," Chris told me while bowing again.

"Is Mr. Salvi the chef?" I asked tartly.

"No, ma'am." Chris shook his head. "However, the chef felt that this dish was better served by Ossetra due to its particular richness of flavor." He leaned forward slightly and dropped his voice to a whisper. "The Chef would not have apologized, ma'am. He believes you will be *quite* happy with the dish as he prepared it."

I smiled. "Of course."

"If you'll excuse me, I'll return with your wine pairing."

"Anyone else both impressed and a little creeped out at the baby godfather's concern about which *caviar* we get served?" Pepper asked, grabbing a small mother-of-pearl spoon. She shoveled a heaping spoonful of the caviar in her mouth.

"Let's be concerned at dessert," Liz told Pepper. "For now, I just want to enjoy this tiny slice of luxury. And not face the fact that I might be *totally* willing to pimp out Fortuna for some oysters and zucchini pearls."

* * *

By the time Chris and his army of waiters brought the Chocolate Truffle Trio nine courses later, I wasn't sure that I wouldn't pimp *myself* out for a meal like this. I popped the Smokey Bacon Truffle in my mouth and pushed out of my mind the fear that I had just traded on Martin's feelings for me.

I was satisfyingly full, and satiated without being stuffed—which seemed bizarre, considering we'd just devoured nine courses of food. My discomfort at the cost of the meal would only give me indigestion.

"Okay, what was your favorite?" Liz asked.

"The Chilean Sea Bass," Miss Bessie said without hesitation.

"The Truffle Tomato Soup with the Crispy Fontana Grilled Cheese," Claire said.

"That was, like, the *least* expensive thing on the menu!" Liz said, aghast. "Fancy comfort food!"

She shrugged. "I'm a simple girl. I like simple things. Besides, it had shaved white truffle on it. It wasn't *that* inexpensive."

Pepper and I looked at one another. "The Smokey Bacon Truffle," we answered at the same time. Everyone laughed.

"That was, really, one heck of an experience,

Fortuna." Liz's laugh trailed off. "Seriously, though. I've wanted to do this for years, and I just never could afford it."

"I don't know what you're thanking me for, it wasn't *my* idea." I faced her. "Besides, you took me here before for a free dinner. You could have ordered the tasting menu whenever you wanted. Evangeline Laroux would have covered it, don't you think?"

"I took you here and got us a *table*," Liz pointed out. "We still got a bill at the end of the night, remember? I can get a *table*, but you got us a spread fit for a table of queens."

"Maybe we should talk about that now that we can't feel guilty, change our minds, and not eat." Pepper turned. "I'm a go with the flow kind of girl, but this is a level of courting that goes *way* beyond polite pressure, Fortuna."

"Besides, *Nosy Parker* over there has turned her sights from my grandson," Miss Bessie said with exasperation. She pointed a bony finger at Pepper. "Now that the two of them have *finally* admitted they do not belong together—something I could have told them both *years* ago, by the way—we need to have a conversation about why a good, steady, down-to-earth boy makes a better husband than a handsome, mysterious millionaire."

"Not that again." I buried my face in my hands.

"That isn't coming up *again*. I just held my tongue out of respect for Gabe while she"—Miss Bessie pointed at Pepper—"had his head all discombobulated."

"Hey, now," Pepper complained.

"What?" the old woman barked.

"How do you even know I'm not interested in Gabe anymore?" Pepper leaned forward and narrowed her eyes toward Miss Bessie. "Maybe I'm keeping him on the back burner as my fall-back guy. *You* don't know."

"I know more than you think," Miss Bessie said, her gravelly voice deadly serious. "You remember that, Pepper Stanford."

Pepper rolled her eyes.

"Wow, *you* can turn on a dime," a tipsy Liz observed. Then she hiccuped.

"You have no idea," Claire whispered without looking up.

This made Miss Bessie pause for a moment and scan the table with her watery eyes. "When you girls have lived a lifetime...when you look back over what you should have done or could have said, or might have tried but didn't, you'll understand why us elder folk are the way we are. Time makes us see things you *can't look at* at your age. Things you don't believe. Things you won't know until it's too late."

We sat silently, staring at the solemn old woman. She met each one of our eyes defiantly.

"Now, I know where my mistakes were." She crossed her arms. "I'm going to use the little bit of my life I got left to try and make sure you don't repeat my mistakes. If I can."

"Everyone has to make their own mistakes, Miss Bessie," I told her across the table softly. "That's just part of life. You just do the best you can as you're faced with the choices that appear in front of you."

"Coming from the woman who avoids choices like the plague."

My face burned hot. "That's not fair! I chose to become a—"

"I have to pee," she complained as she pushed herself up out of the booth with much grunting and grumbling. "Come on, Claire. Let's let them talk about me behind my back."

Claire hurried after her. With one last glare in my direction from Miss Bessie, they left us and walked out of sight.

"What bug crawled up *her* butt and died?" Liz asked, surprised.

"Miss Bessie is frustrated with the pace of progress, I think," Pepper answered. "She and Fortuna are working on a project, and they disagree about the path they should take."

"Gabe?" Liz looked confused.

"No, I think *that* one's my fault." Pepper sighed and pushed her plate of truffles away without finishing the last one. "Bessie was anxious when Gabe and I started wondering whether we should get back together. She's always had some weird idea that Gabe is destined for someone, and it was *never* me."

"You think her whole *Marry Gabe* garbage isn't a joke?" It hadn't occurred to me that Miss Bessie really, truly believed that Gabe and I were somehow magically destined to be together. That the source of the jokes was a deeply held belief. I just assumed she was a crazy old woman playing matchmaker.

"I don't know, Fortuna," Pepper said, and then she sighed. Raising her gaze, she met my eyes. "Years ago, even *I* thought my interest in the paranormal was a little kooky. All the stuff I wrote about on my blog? I don't know if I *really* believed in the stories."

"I know I didn't," Liz said.

"Right? So, I always dismissed her little mystical statements. Hell, I don't even remember half of them. Now?" She shrugged. "It's more true than I ever thought it *would* be, to be honest. Does that mean she's right, or serious, about you and Gabe?"

Pepper fell silent and didn't answer.

As the three of us sat in the immaculate booth that bore no evidence of a nine-course meal having been consumed by five women, I thought about how much I understood.

And how little.

"I don't believe in destiny," I announced after a few moments. "We have choices, all of us. We decide what affects us in our life, what possibilities we grasp. What we let go of and move on from." I nodded. "There is *no* unchangeable destiny. I'm sure of that."

"So, Fortuna?" Liz looked at me and raised her eyebrow. "A leaf doesn't have to *believe* in or understand photosynthesis. It *still* turns green just the same."

* * *

As we left the restaurant, I walked ahead of the group down the long corridor that led away from the Centre Supper Club and back toward the track, casino, and other entertainment contained within the Complex. I was relieved that the Club's proprietor, Evangeline Laroux, had not shown up at our table—one less thing to worry about.

Even so, I felt confused. And frustrated. Martin and I had agreed to be friends. Only friends. His keeping tabs on me, treating us to a lavish dinner for *five* people—

The thought in my head was cut off as I spotted Martin Salvi walking down the sloped hallway toward me.

I turned to the group and pointed to a bench along the side. "Wait here." The four women stopped in surprise, gazed past me, and then sighed as they made their way to the seats.

"Who made *her* Miss Thing?" Miss Bessie grumbled under her breath as Claire helped her toward the bench.

Martin was smiling until he got closer and caught my unhappy expression. His broad smile melted into a frown. When we were about three feet apart, he sighed heavily. "You're upset about the dinner. I can tell."

"I feel like you're trying to *buy* me," I told him.

He shook his head and leaned away as if he was trying to give me physical space. "That wasn't my intention at all, Fortuna. Security mentioned you were on the property, and I just wanted to treat you and the ladies to dinner. That's all."

"It was a multi-thousand dollar dinner!" I told him.

"Yes, Chris did relate to me that you all had chosen our tasting menu," Martin responded with an amused twinkle in his eye. As I opened my mouth to explain, he held up his hand. "Not that I'm bothered by it, mind you—it's a *wonderful* experience, and Chef Jean does a wonderful job. I'm glad I could treat you—but," he said as he leaned forward, "it was *Liz* that chose *that* bit of extravagance. Not something *I* forced upon you. Though don't get me wrong, I was happy to—"

"I can pay for my own dinner!" I protested, changing the subject.

Martin cocked his head and tilted it, raising his eyebrow.

"Okay, maybe not *that* dinner," I admitted, blushing.

"I'm confused. Are you upset because I treated you and your friends to dinner or to a multi-thousand dollar dinner?"

"I...I'm upset because...because...oh, I don't know *why* I'm upset," I told him as I turned away and sat down on one of the benches that lined the walkway. Martin was right. I could have stopped Liz from ordering the most expensive dinner we could have, and I didn't. I could have insisted I pay for dinner, and I didn't. "I'm sorry, Martin. I think I'm just overly sensitive about...stuff. Miss Bessie said some things at dinner, and I wasn't sure what to do. It reminds me of—"

"Say no more." Martin cut me off and kneeled down in front of me. "I apologize if it made you feel uncomfortable. How about we change it up a bit? Come to my house tomorrow. Let *me* cook *you* dinner. Just the two of us. And Gideon, if you like."

"You can cook?" I asked him skeptically.

"I'm Italian," he answered, faintly offended at the question. "Of *course* I can cook."

Martin had never invited me to his home before. He'd been to my shop, and my apartment upstairs, and we'd seen each other here at the Complex. Never once, though, had he invited me over.

"Okay, let's do that," I nodded. He pushed himself to his feet and extended his hand to help me up.

As I turned, I could feel Miss Bessie's glare.

FOUR

Following my phone's navigation directions, I turned onto a private street and nearly drove smack into a large pair of locked metal gates. I squinted at the arch over them.

GRIGIO HILLS

Dropping my gaze, I rolled down the window while inching toward the large brick pillar to the right of the entrance. Buttons shone, and an LED screen lit the area brightly. Before I could get the window halfway down to buzz, the gates opened to let me in.

I frowned, and Gideon barked.

"It just creeps me out sometimes, that's all," I told the dog as I rolled the window back up.

An image of me looking frantically all around me, a paranoid look on my face, appeared in my mind. Then I saw myself encased in an ice block, immobile.

"Don't tell me to chill out," I told the him as I accelerated up the hill. "If I was completely chill and didn't overreact sometimes, *you'd* still be living at the racetrack running around in circles so humans could bet on you, dude."

Gideon whimpered softly.

"Sorry, bud." I took my hand off the steering wheel and scratched him behind the ears. Gideon pressed his head against my side and gave a low, happy yelp. "I wasn't trying to remind you of things that you'd rather forget. Hey, maybe we can convince Martin that having a casino, a strip club, a club, and a dozen restaurants is more than enough, huh?"

Gideon barked in agreement.

We pulled up the winding road through a beautiful canopy of trees covering the driveway like a natural tunnel. Suddenly, the sloping drive flattened out, and we emerged into a large parking lot in front of a massive white modern mansion.

"Holy smokes," I breathed. Gideon barked. "I think this is bigger than my adoptive parents' house in Los Angeles."

Gideon barked again and shoved an image of the large rectangular building to the right. He continued to share his thoughts, imagining dogs walking in and out of it. Then the scene switched to a fantasized interior filled with pools, bacon dispensers, and large soft pillows everywhere for greyhounds to lounge on.

"I don't think it's a doghouse, Gideon. Look at the huge doors," I said as I pointed to the vast, barn-like entrance. "I *think* that's a big garage for fancy cars. See? The road goes right to it."

The dog made a confused sound and tilted his head.

I pulled into a parking space—yes, there were parking spaces—and turned off the van. "Come on, Gideon," I called. The dog hopped over into the driver's seat and then jumped down. His nose twitched in the air as his eyes scanned the bushes for any wayward rabbits he might want to chase. I held tighter to his leash.

"Miss Delphi," an older man called from the front walkway. "Gideon," he nodded formally to the greyhound. "My name is Jerome Watson, Mr.

Salvi's butler. I would be pleased to show you into the kitchen where Martin is"—the butler frowned—"attempting to prepare your meal."

"*Attempting?*" I asked with concern.

"Please follow me, Miss," he said. He turned on his heel and walked stiffly toward the door. "And good luck to you," he murmured under his breath.

Gideon and I followed Jerome through the front yard, through the fancy double doors that had to be ten feet tall, and into a foyer at *least* as big as my store.

* * *

"You came!" Martin said with sweat on his brow. His sleeves were rolled up haphazardly as he stood before a commercial-grade range, stirring a large pot.

"I said I would," I told him as I slid onto a stool across from the range. "You look a little frazzled for someone that insisted they could cook with such certainty."

"I *can* cook. My mother taught me to make all the family recipes when I was younger," he told me. Glancing toward a pan, Martin frowned, and turned up the heat. "What I didn't realize is that I haven't cooked since I moved *here*, and I don't know where anything is or"—he grabbed a pot and picked it up frantically—"how these appliances work."

"Do you have a cook or chef or something?"

"I gave her the night off." Martin frowned again, glancing at the pan. "She's upstairs in her room."

"Why don't you ask for her help?"

"I *told* you I could do this myself, and *that's* what I'm going to do," he responded fiercely. Looking up, Martin seemed embarrassed by his answer. "Sorry. This isn't your fault. I'm just frustrated."

"What are you making?"

"Tagliatelle alla Scala. I know you like mushrooms, so—"

A pot boiled over. Martin cursed and grabbed it.

"*In bianco* or *in rosso*?" I asked, referencing the dish's two versions, one made with heavy cream and another with tomatoes.

He looked up, surprised. "You know the dish?"

"I can't cook, but I *do* eat," I told Martin, feeling somewhat sorry for him as his brows knitted together in frustration. I couldn't cook for the same reason that Martin was having such a hard time in his own kitchen. I grew up having everything done *for* me—and did not, as Martin did, have a mother who felt teaching me to do things on my own was important. "Look, Martin—"

"One second." He grabbed frantically at the pan he had just raised the heat on. It was now smoking, filled with dark, charred vegetables. "You *have* to be kidding me."

"Martin, go see if the cook would be willing to finish the meal, or start over, or whatever needs to be done." I stood up and came around the center island. "Then get us some drinks, let her take over if she's available. You can show me around your home while we wait."

Martin looked for a minute like he would argue, but then he sighed and threw the dish towel down in frustration. "I'm sorry. I really should have practiced a few times before I did this."

"It's fine. Really."

"Jerome, get Adelaide," Martin barked in a commanding tone of voice. "Explain the situation and ask her to finish preparing the meal." Jerome, who had apparently been standing in the hallway, looked in, nodded once, and disappeared.

I frowned. So much for *asking* Adelaide if she would work on her night off. I tried to set my judgment aside, but the way he *demanded* she interrupt her free evening bothered me.

"Let me show you to the sitting room." Martin placed an arm around my back lightly and steered me toward an open area at the end of the kitchen. "I'll run upstairs and get changed, and we can start our evening."

* * *

Minutes later, Martin came down the stairs looking like the sweaty frustration in the kitchen had never happened. His black slacks were perfectly pressed and set off by his stark white silk shirt. His hair even looked slightly damp, as if he had showered. "A glass of wine?" Martin asked as he walked commandingly across the sitting room toward the bar.

"Honestly, just water or iced tea if you have it, please," I told him. He frowned. "I don't really drink that much, and I'm still dehydrated from all the wine last night."

Another frown.

"Am I derailing a plan you had to get me drunk and convince me I should fall into bed with you despite the boundaries we agreed on?" I asked him pleasantly. "A bed I suspect is at *least* king-sized, wrapped in high-end cotton or silk sheets—"

"I wouldn't be averse to the evening taking that direction, Fortuna," he admitted, his frown turning into a charmingly seductive smile.

Gideon growled at him.

"Is there a mirror on the ceiling?"

"No." Martin looked startled for a moment and then composed himself after a long pause. Then he swallowed. "Why, would you *want* one?"

"I could *never* have a romantic relationship with someone so narcissistic that they had a mirror above their bed. Besides, we're friends, right? *Just* friends," I told him as he sat down beside me. I looked around. "No pets?"

"No."

"For some reason, I thought you'd have a cat," I said and sipped my tea. "I also didn't really picture your house like this. It's so...white. White marble flooring, white leather furniture."

"There so much color at work that I like things a little more subdued at home." Martin leaned back and sipped his wine. His steely eyes watched as my gaze traveled around the room and took in the art. "See anything you like?" he asked.

"Yeah, that vase." I pointed as I spotted a vase on prominent display in an alcove off the sitting area. Getting up, I walked over and examined it. "It's a replica of an ancient Egyptian vase or urn, right?"

"That's not a replica." Martin got up to join me. "That's a Marl clay vase from Malqata. I purchased it just a few months ago."

I looked at him suspiciously, expecting he might be joking.

But he wasn't.

Oh, boy.

"Yeah, no, it's a replica, all right," I told him, pointing to a tiny chip in the pottery that exposed a white spot. "See that? Marl clay isn't white when it chips. That's plaster, like from a replica cast."

Martin frowned. "That's not possible, Fortuna. It was graded *and* certified." He leaned forward and squinted at the chip I pointed to. "I paid *thousands* for this vase. From Redlands Antique Auction—it's a *very* reputable auction house. They never would have sold a plaster replica. It just isn't possible."

I had heard of it, and he was right—Redlands would have caught a fake this bad in two seconds. It didn't change that I was entirely sure *this* vase was a fake.

"Martin, that's bleach *bright* white. That's *not* clay," I told him. I got on my toes and looked inside. Then I looked at the outside and spotted a very, very faint line. "Look here, you can even *see* the seam. It's faint, but it's there. This isn't even a *good* replica. Someplace like Redlands would never have sold this like...well, like *this*."

"I don't understand how this is possible."

"Have you had this on display anywhere else?"

"No." Martin shook his head. "Nowhere.

Jerome took the delivery, and as soon as it was delivered, he put it up for display right here. Right on this pedestal." Martin crossed his arms. "Possession went straight from Redlands to me."

"Well, to *Jerome*," I pointed out. "I assume you weren't here when it arrived. How long have you known the butler?"

"Jerome's been with my family since I was young, Fortuna," Martin said of the older butler. "There's no chance that he would be disloyal to my family."

"Okay, then maybe we need to call the police—"

"No. *No* police," Martin told me in a tone that made the statement non-negotiable. "My family has a...thing about involving the police in our personal affairs."

I tilted my head and looked at Martin, surprised at his refusal. He had Chief Clutterbuck on speed dial. Why would he be hesitant about calling the police to investigate? "You deal with the police all the time at the track. Heck, according to Gabe, you guys practically fund the police and built their building and—"

"That's business," he told me. "This is my home. It's different."

"How is it different?"

"It just *is*." His brows knitted together. I waited

for further explanation but got none. "Hey, I have an idea." Martin turned. "Can you help me figure out what happened to the vase? How this replica got here? You specialize in art—"

Me? "Martin, I'm not a forensic investigator—"

"—and you and Pepper have cracked cases the police haven't bothered to investigate," he added, not stopping to listen. "I think we can figure out what happened on our own. There's not much going on at the Complex this week, so I can give my undivided attention to this."

"I have classes this week," I told him, shaking my head. "Besides, you want *Pepper* poking around in your personal affairs?" I asked him, surprised at the suggestion.

"No, I think you and I can figure this out, just the two of us. I'm just pointing out you've had some experience working on cases."

"Just the two of us?"

"Yes."

Gideon leaned against my leg as I stared at Martin, suddenly suspicious of...well, of *him*. I had made it clear to Martin I was only interested in friendship, and he'd made it clear that he was interested in much more. My witchy sense was tingling with a feeling that all was not as it appeared to be here.

"You want the two of us to find out why your

expensive urn has been switched out with a cheap replica?"

Martin nodded. "I do. It might be fun."

* * *

I drove home that night, troubled. Weaving the company van through the winding roads back toward town, I talked to Gideon about my concerns. He was, as you might expect, a pretty good listener.

"He couldn't have set this all up just to make me spend time with him, right?" I asked the dog as I tapped my finger against the steering wheel.

Gideon sent an image of a bandit running away with a vase.

"No, what I mean is...so, okay, there are *three* possible scenarios, right? One, the vase really was stolen, and he's just hypersensitive about having the police in his house and in his personal life because of his dad," I said.

Gideon sneezed.

"That would basically mean everything is as it seems, for the most part, right? But scenario two?" I asked as I came to a stop and checked for traffic in the town square. Finding none, I turned. "Scenario two is he knew it was stolen before I spotted it, and acted surprised tonight just to rope me into looking into it."

Gideon sent the image of a question mark.

"Either because he didn't want the police looking into it, because he didn't want to ask me outright, or because Martin saw he could use it to spend more time with me? I don't know."

Gideon barked three times.

"Three?" I asked him.

He barked once.

"Scenario three is there *is* no missing vase at all," I told the dog as we drove up to the store and parked. "This is all an elaborate scheme to get me to let down my guard and spend more time with him."

Gideon sent me an image of three doors, and a question mark.

"I don't know, pup." I opened the door and got out, standing aside for the spindly-legged hound. "I *wish* I did, but I just don't know."

An image of me leaning into a large chest shaped like Martin's head appeared in my mind. His skull was hinged and open. I was leaning over and frantically rummaging through it, pulling things out and examining them.

"Charlotte said one of the worst things for her with friends and dating was the ability to read people's minds," I told him. "It's one thing to use my ability to tell when people are lying because they may have murdered someone. It's another to use it in relationships. I've never heard of that working out."

I slammed the lid on the Martin-chest. Then Gideon appeared with bacon hanging out of his mouth.

"You know, *I* can buy you bacon, dog. There's nothing special about Martin's bacon."

An image of Martin with plates of bacon. Then of me with a single slice.

"You know, bacon's *not* good for you. A little is fine, but you can't eat a plate of bacon every day. Have *you* ever seen a fat greyhound? I haven't, but you keep eating like that, I just might."

An image of the dog standing on his hind legs, forepaws thrust out in front of him, long snout turned toward the side. Gideon refused to listen to the idea that bacon could be anything but excellent in all ways.

"You know, Gideon, you and I aren't as different as people might think."

The dog barked as we walked in.

FIVE

"Okay, so let me get this straight," Pepper said, sitting on her stool by the counter. "The first time you're in the guy's house, you just *happen* to be shown to a room with a vase. You just *happen* to discover the vase was a fake, he claims it's real, you assure him it's not—but he doesn't want to call the police about it being stolen or faked or whatever? Did I get this right?"

"Yep," I told her as I moved a new painting into the local artists' featured spot in the front of the shop. Azalea Cotton's landscape painting was a beautiful impressionist interpretation of a grove in the nearby mountains, and I thought it would sell quickly. "So, he's either *so* rich that he can blow off an insurance claim for thousands, or this is all some kind of ruse to...well, for whatever reason."

"Or it's stolen," Pepper pointed out.

"Yeah, he could be telling the truth about that, I guess."

"No, I mean it's *stolen*. Like, Martin only *has* it because it's stolen from someone *else*. If it's a stolen piece of art, he wouldn't *want* the police involved." She opened her laptop and typed. "Redlands, right?"

"Yep."

I could hear the chime of incoming email as Pepper typed away on the computer keyboard. "Found it," she announced in less than thirty seconds. Turning the laptop toward me, she raised her eyebrow. "That's a *quarter of a million-dollar* Egyptian urn. Was bought at auction three months ago. That, at least, tracks with what Martin said."

"There is no way to find out if he's the buyer, though," I said as I leaned forward and squinted. "Says the buyer was anonymous."

Pepper rolled her eyes. "Like *that's* going to stop us. I just so happen to know someone that can hack into anything."

"I think Ollie's *technically* the police, though."

"You want to find out if Martin bought it himself or not?" Pepper asked, rolling her eyes again, this time in apparent exasperation. "You know, I don't get you sometimes." Pepper circled her head as if her neck was tense. "You're one of the smartest people I know—present company excluded, of course—but you seem to have these big, *gigantic* blind spots."

Gideon barked.

"I do not! And you," I glared at the dog, "be quiet."

"You do," she disagreed. "What I don't get is *why* you have them. You don't really want to check into your boyfriend. You don't really want to check into the *mystic* thing. You don't really want to check into your birth parents. If I were you and I didn't know who my *parents* were—"

"See, that's just *it. I know* who my parents were," I answered with a frown. "My parents were David and Roberta Addington of Los Angeles, California. They raised me—well, if you could *call* it that. They're all I know. And I grew up knowing they were *unhappy* with the daughter that they paid for. I'm not eager to rush into another situation without...Look, I'm just not ready. End of story."

Pepper looked startled. "You've never told me your adoptive name. Well, your adoptive parents' names."

"You didn't know my original name?" I asked her skeptically.

"Oh, I *knew* it. You've just never *told* me."

Gideon sat quietly, looking back and forth between us.

"I'm two people," I told her. "And reconciling that? It's *not* as easy as you would think."

"We *all* have sides to our personality, Fortuna."

I sat down on the stool behind the cash register and took a deep breath. "You don't understand. I'm actually *legally* two people. I have two birth certificates, one as a foundling with unknown parents—I assume—that's sealed up in some Arkansas courthouse. *Another* stating that David and Roberta Addington are my parents. That my adoptive mother gave *birth* to me. Think about that. The paper that proves my existence? That *paper* is a *lie. You* try starting your very existence when the paper that proves who you are is a lie."

"That's just a piece of *paper*, Fortuna."

"It's a piece of paper that says I'm Heather Anne Addington, daughter of a wealthy pharmaceutical scion. And that's who I was raised to be, even though I never quite fit," I told her. "It's not really *wrong*. That's who I *tried* to be for a very long time."

"So, what happened?" Pepper asked. "Why do you feel like you didn't fit? I mean, lots of us think our parents don't care from time to time—why are you *so* convinced yours didn't?"

"When I turned twelve, my parents started

sending me to boarding schools," I explained as I gazed off toward the front window. "It's easy to disconnect from people that you don't have a lot of contact with." I shrugged. "By the time I was fifteen, I was miserable. No friends because I didn't fit in with the rich girls, no family to emotionally support me because they just weren't those kinds of people. A failure as a daughter. I was nothing like they expected or hoped for."

"I'm so sorry, Fortuna," Pepper said softly, her eyes pained. "No one should grow up in a house where they don't feel loved and supported by their family."

"I was just another possession," I told her, shrugging. "Like, Mother couldn't get pregnant, so she bought a baby."

Pepper's brows knitted together. "Are you some kind of black-market baby?"

"No, nothing like that, it was just...like I was an accessory, you know? Not a *daughter*. Just something to trot out and show off because they were expected to have one. I don't know, I don't know how I got on this topic," I said as I wiped a tear away and cleared my throat. "Everything worked out eventually." I smiled. "I found the Langdon circus, found other people like me, with abilities like mine."

Pepper's eyes suddenly widened. "Oh, my gosh."

"What?"

"You were psychic when you were growing up," she whispered. I nodded. "Were you able to read exactly what your parents thought about you?" I nodded. "Did they know?" I shook my head no. "Oh, Fortuna," Pepper said sympathetically. "That's how you know how they felt. And that's why you have such a hard time rummaging around in people's heads."

"They shouldn't have been parents," I told her. "But, yes. It takes me a little longer to warm up to people. To trust people. And there are things that, maybe, I don't want to find out *just* yet. Maybe I just want to be *happy* for a while. Feel connected to people. Take them at their word. And if they're lying, I don't want to know sometimes. Is that so wrong?"

"It's not what *I* would do, but I had a good family that loved me," Pepper admitted, tilting her head. "I don't know that there's a right and wrong for how you, or anybody, *should* be in this context."

"The circuses were a perfect experience for me," I told her. "I learned about family, *real* family, for the first time. But it was like a fantasy, you know?"

Pepper nodded.

"This? This place? This is something I'm building for *me*. For the first time, *I'm* piecing my own life together. And I don't want my powers or people's inner secret thoughts to dictate my future. I want to make my own choices. Like everyone else."

Pepper shook her head yes. "I think I understand. Well, maybe not completely. But I empathize—and I want you to know how honored I am that you've chosen to trust me as a friend. Especially considering your past."

I nodded, unable to speak.

"I have one more thing to say," Pepper said, her voice thick with emotion.

"Yes?"

"Your roots are showing," she said, pointing to my hair in breaking the air of seriousness that had descended upon us. "You need to visit Liz. Like, now, girl. Roots are for trees, *not* hair."

No one knew that my blonde hair was thanks to a spell I had learned back at the Magical Midway. I decided I would keep that secret to myself for the moment. I was having enough issues with the tourists showing up for readings.

I was surprised to find I felt better having shared with Pepper. She and I had spent so much time with each other over the past few months that we *seemed* like the best of friends, but it felt like we had just taken a giant leap forward toward true friendship.

I had let my guard down. A little bit.

* * *

Ollie walked in a few hours later carrying a laptop case and looking confident. "Okay, what you want me to hack?"

"I have customers here!" I glared at him.

"Awesome. I'm glad business is doing well." Ollie smirked. "I'll set up in your kitchen upstairs. Pepper? You want to come with?"

"Are you sure?" Pepper asked, fluttering her eyelashes. My jaw dropped watching her attempt at coquettishness. "I don't want to *distract* you or anything." She leaned forward and yanked her shirt down to show off her ample cleavage.

Some people, like Martin, flirted as naturally as they breathed.

Pepper was *not* one of those people.

"I could do this with my eyes closed." Ollie waved her enthusiastically toward him. "Come on, I might need your help to know exactly what I'm looking for once I'm in, anyway. Fortuna, you mind if I grab some lunch out of your fridge?"

"I'll make you a sandwich!" Pepper told him racing toward the back.

"*That* girl couldn't be *more obvious* if she jumped on him like a duck on a June bug," a sultry voice said from the doorway. I turned and found, much to my chagrin, that Evangeline Laroux had stopped by my humble art studio.

Ugh. Just what I needed.

"Angie." I nodded. "How can I help you?"

"Well, I've heard tell that you found a way to keep Martin away from the Complex this week," she drawled, walking toward the counter. She headed toward me with the same deliberateness as a model walks the catwalk. Her perfume grew stronger, nearly knocking me off my feet. "He's been runnin' around all morning settin' the place up to run without him and crowin' like a rooster at dawn about *you*."

"I'm not sure I know what you're talking about."

"Now, you listen here," the overly made-up woman hissed as she curled her back and thrust her face forward toward me. It was so close I could count the clumps of mascara on her thick eyelashes. "You *had* your chance when he first got here. While you were gallivanting about town almost getting yourself shot, Martin and I were—"

I held my hand up. "Let me stop you right there. Martin and I *don't* have a romantic relationship, and I have *no* interest in hearing what you and Martin were doing at *any* point in time. Not the past, not currently, and not in the future. It's none of my business."

"I find it *refreshing* that you and I can agree that Martin Salvi is none of your business. I guess even a blind hog can find an acorn once in a while," Evangeline Laroux told me, her tone as cold her icy, rich-husband murdering heart, no doubt.

"I have to ask. Is it just that Martin's the wealthiest guy in town, or something else?" I asked her curiously.

"I'm *in love* with Martin, you presumptuous *witch*."

I chuckled at the ironic insult. "Good for you."

"He could *never* be happy with a plain Jane like you."

"Oh, Evangeline," I said as I leaned forward. My invasion of her space caused her to back up. "You have *no idea* just how plain Jane I'm *not*." I sniffed the air in front of her and caught the heavy scent of alcohol. A smell she was no doubt trying to mask with the gallons of perfume she had doused herself in. "At least I'm sober at lunchtime. Something you don't seem to be capable of."

"I'm warning you, Delphi," Evangeline said, her tone menacing.

I sighed heavily. "Great, you warned me. Nice

job. Unless you want some art supplies or to buy a painting, consider the goal of your visit accomplished." I paused and waited for her to say something. She didn't. Seconds ticked by. Then a few more. All the while, she stared at me, her eyes narrowed. Finally, I lost patience. "You can go now."

"I'll go when I'm good and ready!"

"Anytime you happen to pass my store, I'd sure appreciate it."

Angie blinked, confused. Then, finding the insult in the statement, her eyes narrowed, and her rage blossomed full springtime.

"Martin Salvi *better* be back at work tomorrow," she breathed, and I coughed from the alcohol and perfume miasma that seemed to wrap me in an invisible embrace and was now attempting to crawl down my throat. "He's acting like he's going on vacation with you or somethin', and I won't *have* it." She balled her fists up and took a deep breath. "*Won't* have it!" she screeched.

Just as I was about to let loose on her, I remembered Miss Bessie's observation she was destined to turn out this way. I never heard the story.

My anger softened. Most people never heard my story, either.

There were reasons, always reasons, people

were the way they were. It didn't *excuse* their behavior. But sometimes it made it understandable.

Miss Bessie was right. As annoying as this woman was, she was more pathetic than anything else.

"Angie, I can tell you with a hundred percent certainty that I currently have no romantic interest in Martin Salvi—"

"Good, because he doesn't have any in you!"

"Then everything should work out fine," I told her, shrugging. "You have nothing to worry about."

The concept of having nothing to worry about seemed to be a new one to Evangeline Laroux. Confusion played across her makeup-caked face for a second time, and then the woman looked so pleased that I feared she might break her arm patting herself on the back.

"Yeah, well—" Evangeline Laroux pulled herself up to full height. "Let's *keep* it that way!" She turned on her stiletto heel and stomped toward the front door.

The chime signaled an end to the confrontation.

For now.

* * *

"He bought it, all right," Ollie said with a nod. "It was a legit sale. Least, as far as I can tell."

"Ollie got into that system in less than *five* minutes," Pepper bragged, smiling. "It's like he's a computer superhero or something!"

"Well, I wouldn't go *that* far," he smiled, blushing slightly at Pepper's heaped-on praise.

"He's also *got* an insurance policy on it," Ollie said, and he brought up in the image of a contract on his computer. "It's insured for theft, so I don't get why he doesn't want to call the police. If it is stolen, he *can't* collect on it without a report."

I frowned.

"You really think he's just making all this up to spend time with you?" Ollie asked me. I glared at Pepper. "Oh, don't get upset with her. Anyone could've put two and two together once they heard *this* story. She didn't say anything, but I'd guess that was something you were afraid of."

"I don't know if *afraid* is the right word. I just don't...I don't know if I can trust him. And there are different levels of trust. I guess I'm trying to figure out at *which* level I can trust Martin and which level I can't."

"I hear you," Ollie said. He looked up at me and grinned. "You know, Gabe might be able to help you with that. He's got a lot of information on

Martin. Got it after he helped Salvi check out whether anything at the Complex was crooked."

"Martin was really clear that he didn't want the police involved."

"You're not getting the *police* involved," Ollie pointed out. "You're talking to a friend about a situation. Getting *consultation* on a case from a professional detective. Seems legit to me."

"You should talk to Miss Bessie, too," Pepper added.

"Why?"

"You could practice that scrying thing on this. Besides, if Martin is really doing this just to manipulate time alone with you? What better way to thwart that? Invite the whole gang to participate!"

"If he is doing this to spend time with her, we'll all be about as welcome as an outhouse breeze, Pepper," Ollie said.

"I kind of suggested that last night already," I let them both know. "He was pretty insistent that it be just us."

"*Was* he now?" Ollie said skeptically, his eyebrow raised.

"Who's making *all kinds* of decisions for herself now without being *controlled* by someone else?" Pepper asked innocently, then blinked exaggeratedly several times. She swiveled her head around, scanning the room. When her eyes landed on me, she held her hands out. "Oh! It's you! Miss *no one's going to control me*! Nice to see you!"

Ollie chuckled.

Gideon barked, but I swear, that dog was laughing.

SIX

I was sweeping the floor of the store when Martin walked in, a broad smile on his face.

"Good afternoon!" Jeeves trailed him as he crossed the storefront and leaned in toward me. Before he could pucker his lips, I quickly jerked the broom up and placed it between us. "Ready for our adventure?"

"You make it sound like we're heading out for a hike in the Ouachitas."

"I feel like that a bit. You and Pepper always seem like you're having such fun when you're tracking down something. I guess I'm just excited to get started. And, of course," he smiled, "for the recovery of my urn."

"I don't know if I'd call it *fun*. Anyway, Azalea

should be here in a few minutes," I told him. "She can handle watching the store for the afternoon. Once she's here, we'll head upstairs and see what Pepper and Ollie have found so far."

That got his attention, and he frowned. "I thought it was just the two of us?"

"Yeah, I know what you said, but I thought about it once I got home, and I don't think that's wise." I turned and walked the broom back to the closet and shoved it in. "Pepper and Ollie have some skills that I don't, access to information I don't. We've really only solved stuff when working together. I'm pretty sure we'll find out what happened to your urn faster if they help."

Martin looked straight at me. "*Just* Ollie and Pepper?"

"I'm not sure what you mean," I answered—even though I knew what he meant.

"Where's Gabe?" Martin asked. He had leaned closer toward me *and* lowered his voice as if speaking Gabe's name too loud might call up the detective from wherever he was hiding.

"I don't know." I shrugged. Then, just to be cheeky, I leaned toward Martin and whispered back, "Where's Gabe?" Martin's eyes narrowed as he realized I was toying with him a little bit, and I tried not to laugh.

"You're not *seriously* going to tell me you're considering going out with that man."

"That was a *hell* of a jump from one subject to another, Mr. Salvi. I'm not seriously going to tell you anything about Gabe, to be honest." I shrugged and walked back toward the counter to grab a dust rag. "Again, you and I are friends. He and I are friends. I'm not *dating* anyone. Not you. Not him. The only man in my bed is Gideon, and there's no room for anyone else."

Like, *seriously,* no room for anyone else. That greyhound splayed out on my bed like a spider at the center of a web. Sometimes it felt like he had as many limbs, too.

"You're right." Martin nodded, still standing in the middle of the room. "Of course, you're right."

Talking with Martin about Gabe sometimes felt like a fencing match. Like he would push forward where he knew he had agreed not to go just to test my defenses.

"By the way, Evangeline Laroux dropped in this morning." I headed back around toward the front of the store to dust off the shelves of art books. "She warned me to stay away from you, and that you needed to show up tomorrow *or else.*"

"Or else what?" His eyes looked troubled.

"She didn't get to that part."

The glance between Martin and Jeeves didn't

last longer than a second at the most, but I caught it. Concern on both of their faces.

"*What* was that?" I asked him.

"What was what?"

"That look between you and Jeeves." I pointed back and forth between them. "That look seemed to imply you know why she showed up here. Is there something I should know?" Another glance between them. "Martin, if you ever sit alone at night, your favorite Scotch in hand, *wondering* why I don't agree to go out with you romantically? My advice is to think back to *this* exchange."

"Angie is just jealous, that's all," Martin said. He walked toward me, but I held up my hand.

"I got that. *She* told me that. Well, more or less," I told him.

The doorbells rang as Azalea walked in, looking sweaty and tired. "I'm so sorry I'm late!"

I looked at my phone. "Azalea, you're *five* minutes late."

"I know, I know! I'm so sorry! I had to run to a meeting about—" Her eyes widened as Martin turned around to face her. "Um. Never mind. It was just a meeting, and it ran late." Her eyes dropped as she scurried around the millionaire and his armed guard. "Sorry. It won't happen again."

"Five minutes isn't late, Azalea. You're fine. Hey, you mind watching the shop on your own this afternoon?" I asked her as she shoved her backpack behind the counter. "I have something I need to look into."

"Yeah, no, that'd be awesome! I have some sketches I've been working on," she told me, pulling out several sketchbooks. "This would be a great time to work on it. Besides, Zach Jonson might stop by this afternoon, and this would be a great time to talk to him. You know, alone." The young woman grinned and blushed.

"June Johnson's kid?" Azalea nodded. "The one that goes to the Rhode Island School of Design?" Azalea nodded again. "I haven't met him yet, but a number of the townsfolk told me about him. RISD is no slouch of a school—he must be outstanding."

"I know," she said, almost sighing dreamily. "He posted on the unofficial high school group about being back in town, and he's *really* excited about *Mystic Moon*. I'm *hoping* he comes in to check me—um, it—out."

"Well, then let me get out of here." I smiled at her and waved to Martin. "I'll be upstairs for now if you need me."

* * *

"Come here," Pepper hissed, grabbing my arm and dragging me forcefully into my bedroom.

"Ow! What the heck?"

"*Why* did you bring *him* up here? I thought you were going to investigate with him. Then *we* were going to, you know, *secretly* investigate him behind his back?"

"*You* were the one doing the whole dramatic *who's not being* controlled dance last night," I pointed out. "If I'm on some journey of self-determination, I've determined that I *don't* want to be some sneaky, backstabbing liar."

"It was *your* suggestion!" Pepper was just short of incredulous.

"What does it matter?"

"I had an *entire* plan of attack mapped out for this, and now I have to throw it *all* out the window," she pouted and crossed her arms. "I didn't account for the fact that Martin would be *in* the room with us as we're doing all this!"

"Look, if he really did do this just to spend time alone with me, I don't want to give him that win. I don't like being manipulated like that."

"Right, but—"

"Besides, it'll be a lot more informative to see what his reaction is when we start looking into things, won't it?

"Right, but—"

"Pepper, he's *here* already. He knows what we're doing. What do you want me to do, tell him that we decided not to bother?" I raised an eyebrow as her mouth snapped closed, and she pouted more.

"But it was such a *good* plan," she murmured.

"That involved you and Ollie looking into things alone, no doubt," I guessed.

"Well..." Pepper narrowed her eyes. "Okay, fine. Maybe that had a little bit to do with it."

"Don't manipulate him," I warned her. "Just *tell* him how you feel."

"Oh, hell, no." She shook her head vigorously.

I sighed. "Fine, but *don't* manipulate Ollie. If you two do wind up together, you don't want a relationship to start with secrets and lies and machinations," I told her, glancing at Martin. "Trust me on this one. It can ruin everything."

"I was *completely* honest with Gabe, and look how *that* turned out." Pepper turned away and stomped back over toward the table.

"You were *freshman* in high school," I pointed out.

"And?"

I shook my head and followed her out.

* * *

"So, I looked at the CCTV footage from Redlands, the loading dock at the auction house, and the offloading at Martin's," Ollie said as we sat around the table.

"Wait a minute, *how* are you able to see video footage at *my* house?" Martin asked, jerking his head toward the laptop. "My security system is top-of-the-line. It's supposed to be impenetrable."

"You *might* want to ask for your money back," Ollie told him, turning the computer in Martin's direction. "There's a back door installed. A pretty big one, too. It took me less than five minutes to get in and find the footage I needed."

Martin rubbed his forehead and then rose from his seat to bark for Jeeves down the staircase. "This is absolutely unacceptable," he said, whirling back around.

"Dude, calm down," Ollie told him. "I can patch the thing in about *three* minutes, but whoever installed your computer system? You might not want to use them again. I don't know if this back door is for the security company to access, or someone stuck it in there to be able to get footage on you, but you may want to find out."

"You can patch it?" Martin waved Jeeves back.

The taciturn security took his place against the wall to stand watch over our group.

"Can. If you trust me to," Ollie shrugged. "You may want to have someone that works—"

"You do it. Patch it."

"Okay, give me a sec."

We all sat silently as Ollie typed, and Martin fumed. His eyes flashed with anger as he shared another knowing look with Jeeves, and I wondered again what the two weren't telling us. Martin had not explained to him what had transpired, *or* why he was so angry. Somehow, Jeeves *seemed* aware, anyway.

I stared at the tall armed guard again. He looked human, he *seemed* human.

As if he sensed my silent examination, Jeeves turned and stared into my eyes. His gaze was intense, dark eyes almost mesmerizing as we looked at one another.

All I had to do was take a peek. Just open myself up to him, see what energy he threw off.

Just a peek.

"Done," Ollie told Martin. "Feel free to have that double checked by someone you trust if you want, but that back door has been closed, locked, *and* barricaded. No one's getting through there."

"Can you find out who did it?"

"*That* would take a little bit more time. It just depends on what you want me to focus on. Your urn, or the back door hack." Ollie looked at Martin, his expression questioning.

Martin's deep brown eyes seemed troubled as several looks passed back and forth between him and Jeeves, but he finally shook his head no. "We're trying to focus on the urn, so let's do that."

"Right, so as I was saying," Ollie hit a few keys and brought up three windows with film footage. "Because of the insurance at Redlands, they keep a video camera on their items until they're delivered. As far as I can tell, none of this footage has been messed with. The urn was sold at Redlands," he pointed, "loaded into that truck," he pointed again, "and delivered to your house."

"How can you tell it's the urn and not the fake?" Pepper asked him.

"The appraiser examined it before it got loaded up," Ollie hit a few more keys and pulled up a crystal clear video of a stern looking man in a suit examining the urn with a magnifying glass. After a minute or two, he nodded, and several burly men packed it up in a box. "Fortuna knows more about this than I do, but Pepper said that Fortuna told her Redlands has an excellent reputation."

"They do. They're one of the top antiquities auction houses in the country. There is no way they would have shipped a counterfeit. I just can't see it happening. It's not *impossible*, but it seems unlikely."

"For the moment, I think we should assume you bought the real thing, and they shipped the real thing. Sure, it's *possible* that the switch happened at

Redlands, but that's going to be *much* harder to investigate. At this point," Pepper said, "I think we should assume the switch happened at Martin's and start there."

I nodded. "Well, that's easy, then, right? Martin has a security system that videos the house. Let's just check the footage."

"That's a couple of months and a *lot* of hours," Ollie said. "I'm going to have to string together all of it, then write some kind of algorithm that picks out motion. Unless you have motion sensors?" Martin shook his head no.

"The video surveillance system runs all the time. It records everything."

"Yeah, so, that's a bigger job," Ollie nodded. "I'm gonna need my desktop. This laptop might not have the processing power or the disk space to hold that, especially if all of it is in HD."

"Okay, so, Ollie and I will go to his house and check out the footage. Fortuna, you and Martin should go to his house and examine the room. See if you can spot anything. Check out the replica, too. Maybe we can figure out who made it."

In five sentences, Pepper had manipulated alone time for her and Ollie, and me and Martin.

I had no doubt she did it on purpose.

"You're *only* going to look at that video, right?" Martin asked. His mouth set in a hard-line as he stared at Ollie. "Not that I don't trust you," he added politely, "but this is my *home*. There's obviously going to be stuff on the surveillance video I would...prefer remain private."

I raised my eyebrow, but Martin didn't look at me.

"I'm *not* gonna violate the bro code, dude, don't worry," Ollie responded.

"*I* don't have a bro code," Pepper told Martin.

"And I don't have any qualms about turning you both in for breaking into my security system if you violate my trust," Martin told Pepper as she gave him a lopsided grin.

"I can do the bro code for a day."

"Splendid."

SEVEN

Jeeves was out of the driver's side and around the vehicle to open our door in the blink of an eye. As he reached out his hand to help me onto the driveway, his skin was smooth and cool. My eyes drifted up to his face. A clean-shaven face. Almost preternaturally polished.

"Whatever cleanser you use does a *fantastic* job, Jeeves," I told him while waiting for Martin to get out of the limo. "I'd love to know what it is. Your skin is so tight that I can't even see any pores!" I pointed to my own skin and rolled my eyes. "Clearly, *I* could use some help. What's your skin regimen?"

"Do you really think we have time to discuss

beauty secrets, Fortuna?" Martin asked. He nodded quickly at Jeeves and jerked his head toward the house. The body man turned quickly, walking away from us without answering my question.

"Lethal skills, fantastic skin, barely sleeps," I ticked off, making my way toward the sidewalk. "Where did you find him?" I shielded my eyes from the bright morning, glancing up at Martin. His jaw muscle was twitching. "Did he work for your father's family first, or did you hire him?"

Martin pulled away from me, his steps getting faster in a beeline toward the door. Once there, he entered a code into the electronic door lock. "Here we are." Stepping back, he held it open like a gentleman—but didn't respond to my question.

I know I've mentioned before that Jeeves seldom spoke, and he was rarely far from Martin's side. Initially, I *thought* he was just one of those still waters run deep kinda guys. Or, like one of those Secret Service agents you see walking around the president. Their eyes scan like sharks looking for chum in the water, but they rarely talk and have learned how to fade into the background. As if they weren't even there. Maybe ...

But Martin said his family had dealt with paranormals before. Knew of them...us. So it could be more than that, too. I mean, when did the guy *sleep?*

Ugh. For someone who *wanted* to take people at face value, I had my moments of suspicion.

"That's very frustrating, you know," I told Martin with genuine annoyance.

"I'm sorry? I didn't hear your question," Martin lied. He walked purposefully through the hallway toward the back of the house where the alcove and replica were.

"Then how do you know it was a question?"

Martin dipped his head slightly, his back still toward me. With a low voice, he murmured, "Touché, Ms. Delphi."

And that was that. He didn't circle back and actually *answer* the darn thing.

"Mr. Salvi, sir, I didn't know that you were going to be home so early," a rotund woman in a paisley dress said with an accent I couldn't quite place. She hustled out of the kitchen, wiping her wet hands on her apron. "Will you be wantin' me to fix you and your lady friend lunch, then, sir?"

"That would be wonderful, Adelaide, but not right away. Fortuna and I have some work to do before we can sit down and take a break."

"You are Ms. Delphi, the art lady, then?" Adelaide asked, her eyes wide. "It's very good to make your acquaintance, miss." The gray-haired woman eyed me up and down as if taking my measure, but didn't extend her hand to shake. "Is there anything you can't eat, miss? Anything you might be allergic to?"

Her gaze made me feel like a butterfly pinned to a board *despite* her kindly expression. "Nope, I can eat pretty much anything."

"I can attest to that," Martin joked with a smirk.

"Well, you just call me Addie, then, and if you need anything, I'll be in my kitchen." The sunny old woman nodded as she straightened her apron and turned to leave us alone.

"You certainly seem to need a lot of house staff for someone who's hardly ever here."

Martin raised his eyebrow. "Are we going to have the money disagreement again?"

I frowned. "What money disagreement?"

"The uncomfortable conversation where you make fun of the fact that I have money. A conversation that *sometimes* turns your lighthearted banter into an unspoken implication that you're slightly better than me. Because you walked away and left it all behind."

"You're completely wrong about that."

"Oh?" Martin asked with an eyebrow raised.

"I don't feel like I'm better than you, Martin," I told him in a relaxed tone. "But I do disagree with *this* level of excess. It's bordering on obscene."

Martin's face reflected a serenity that seemed forced. His jaw muscle twitched.

"Look, it's not a judgment on you as a *person*," I said as I waved away any possible sting of my previous comment. "I honestly think there's such a thing as *too* much money. I mean, *look* at this house. You're *one* person, Martin. Does one person really need *this* much space?" I gestured toward the rest of his considerable mansion.

The house had to be at least six bedrooms. Maybe more. We had passed two dining rooms and one living area on the way in. A wet bar. I wasn't even bringing up the large garage that Gideon had hoped was a monstrously sized greyhound day spa.

"I don't need this much space, but why is it such a problem for you that I have it? If I can afford it?" he asked me.

It annoyed me that Martin's eyes were more amused by my statement than interested in my viewpoint. But he asked me a question, and so I answered—maybe I could show him how that was done. "It's a problem for me when *anybody* has so much, and other people have so little."

"I have to admit the argument is somewhat droll coming from you. Wasn't it *you* just a few days ago getting a twenty-five hundred dollar meal with your friends?" Ouch. That stung. As I opened my mouth to protest, he added, "You said *excess*. So, is your issue that I'm not philanthropic enough?"

"No, I don't know what you do for charity—"

"That's right," he cut me off coldly and crossed his arms. "You don't. You don't know why I am living this way. You don't know why I'm doing what I'm doing. If you ever get down off your high horse for two seconds, I *might* even tell you."

My jaw dropped. Was he serious? "You know, it's not like I haven't *asked*. Repeatedly. Don't get on me for making a judgment based on what I know, and then giving me guff about what I *don't*. I've asked. *You* won't tell me."

As if Addie could sense things in the room were getting tense, she swept in with a tray of tea, coffee, and tiny cucumber sandwiches. "I know you said it's not the time for lunch, but *surely* you two need a morning snack and some tea, yes?" Without waiting for an answer, the cook began pouring cups and arranging small plates.

"I have to admit, I *am* feeling a bit peckish," I admitted, reaching for a cup.

* * *

"Every artist signs their work," I told him as I went over the replica inch by inch by inch. "It may not be obvious, but there's always some telltale sign. But no matter how many times I look at this thing, I can't see it."

"Look, I'm sorry about before—"

I sighed in frustration. Between his tendency to not answer a question and my tendency to change the subject when I was annoyed? The likelihood of this ever turning into a romantic relationship was so low as to be practically non-existent. I sat back from the fake urn and stretched, rolling my shoulders to get the kinks out of them.

"Martin, you have to understand that I have my own viewpoints. I have my own history. I had experiences that colored my viewpoint long before I ever met you. Some of my views have nothing whatsoever to do with you at all." He nodded. "I'm open to having my mind changed, I really am," I said. I leaned away from the replica and turned to face him. "But you have to understand the better I get to know you, the *more* questions I have, and—to be frank—the more evasive you seem about answering them. You're expecting a lot without giving much"

"But I—"

"Bacon doesn't count."

"*This* is why I don't try to have a relationship," Martin said, and then sighed heavily. "Look, just like there are things that you didn't feel like you could tell me? I have things that I don't feel like I can tell you. Not yet."

"First, we're *not* in a relationship. We're friends." Martin frowned. "Second, does Gabe know these things you feel you can't tell me?" Martin didn't like Gabe, and if Gabe knew the things Martin refused to tell me, that would really make me question this friendship and its future.

"I *told* you who my father was. That was a big leap of faith for me, you know. Telling you and the rest where I came from. It's where I *came* from, though, Fortuna. It's not who I *am*."

"And I appreciated the trust. Honestly, it went a long way with me. Even if it doesn't seem like it," I admitted.

"But?"

"Look, I'm a telepath, okay? Telepath, psychic, empath—whatever you want to call it. Even when I rein it in, even when I do my *absolute best* to respect people's privacy and not go rummaging around in their minds...I *still* have a sixth sense. A feeling that's not really magic, but that is...that is *beyond* the realm of logic," I explained. "Can you understand what I mean?"

"A little bit, yes," he answered. "Like an instinct."

"I have respected your privacy as much as I can. I have not gone into your mind and tried to pluck out things I know you're hiding from me. But I

know you're hiding things from me," I told him.
"Not just that you're hiding things, but hiding
things from *me*. Whether it's because you don't
trust me, whether it's because you think I would be
angry or think less of you? I don't know."

His eyes searched mine, and then they widened
in surprise. "You think I'm hiding things from you
because of you."

I nodded. "I do. And as long as I have that
feeling?"

"I don't have a chance with you," Martin
concluded.

"*What* is Jeeves?" I asked him point blank.

He stared at me, unblinking.

"Is he human? Is he a paranormal?"

Silence.

I threw up my hands. "Man, seriously? Look,
you've got my answer. This? This romantic thing
that you seem to want? This is in your hands. Not
mine. Maybe that's disappointing to you, but it's the
truth. Now, I suggest we stop focusing on the two of
us and start focusing on your urn if you ever want to
get it back."

Martin glanced down for a moment and then
took a deep breath. Looking up, he smiled sadly and
nodded. "Thank you for helping me with this."

"Don't thank me. I haven't done anything yet."

* * *

We set aside the...discussion? Confrontation? And focused on the lost art. I combed through Martin's alcove area for clues as Martin trailed me, answering questions. If there *was* any evidence, I wasn't able to spot anything.

Mid-afternoon, Martin asked Jerome, his butler, to prepare a list of companies and people that had been inside the house since the urn had been delivered.

"Excellent, sir. Do you wish to have *all* people, sir?" he asks knowingly, his eyes narrowed. "Or just contracted people?"

"Well, now that you said it like *that*, Jerome, if I tell you to only concentrate on contractors, Fortuna here will *assume* I'm hiding something from her."

I said nothing.

He wasn't wrong.

"As complete a list as you can, Jerome," Martin answered finally. "Oliver Kane has obtained the security footage from the house and is, as we speak, splicing it together so we can examine the movements of everyone in the house."

Jerome's eyes opened wide in alarm. "I'm sorry, sir. Did you say he *obtained*, sir?"

"Apparently, we had a back door installed in our security system."

"A back door, sir?"

"A way for somebody to come into our systems whenever they wanted to. Mr. Kane has patched the hole in the system, but we'll want to look into that."

"Yes, sir. I can do that today if you wish, sir?"

I had watched seasons of *Star Trek* that contain the word *sir* less.

"Let's wait on that, Jerome. But I do want you to go all the way back to when the system was installed. As far as who's been in the house, I mean."

"Yes, sir." Jerome nodded sharply and turned. Pausing, he glanced back at Martin. "Do you want that in one list, or two, sir?'

Martin glared at his butler and then glanced at me.

"Clearly, just one list, Jerome. Because, again," he said with forced joviality. "You've kind of boxed me into a corner here."

"My apologies, sir."

"That'll be all, Jerome."

"Yes, sir."

I wondered why Martin's butler had so *clearly* painted him into a corner. Martin seemed sure that the people who worked for him were loyal to him, but Jerome could have easily asked him those questions in private. As I mused over the exchange,

I caught Addie standing in the archway of the kitchen, arms crossed, and a puzzled look on her face.

Apparently, I wasn't the only one wondering why Jerome had burned Martin.

EIGHT

The store was relatively quiet when we returned. Azalea looked up briefly from her sketchbook, smiled, and quickly returned her attention to whatever she was working on. "They are upstairs," she said without looking up again, her pencil scratching wide arcs on the paper. "Zach didn't stop by yet. *If* he will. Which, I mean...*Maybe* he won't. But *I* still think he will."

"An art student from a prestigious university *not* checking out the first art studio in his hometown? Impossible. *I* think it's a safe bet he will stop by at some point," I told her.

"Is that your psychic intuition talking?" Azalea looked up and grinned.

"That's my *artist's* intuition." I winked at her.

"By the way, you don't mind if I work extra hours, do you?" the teenager wanted to know. "My work-study's only scheduled for four hours a day, but with the twins at home, it's hard to get *any* quiet so I can concentrate. I get *lots* of quiet here." Azalea told me about her rambunctious siblings, seven-year-old identical twins Alder and Anthony. "I love the boys, but they're *really* loud."

"You *sure* your request has to do with Alder and Anthony?" I teased her.

"Well, I mean, *obviously*, if I hang out here, the mathematical probability *alone* says I stand a better chance of running into Zach," she admitted, blushing. "I mean, if you *don't* need me, you don't have to pay me to watch the shop. I'll just—"

"Nonsense." I waved off her concern. The front doorbell rang, and I turned to see Martin coming in behind me "It would work out for me, too. Martin and I are—"

"Just taking the week to spend some time together," Martin interjected, cutting me off. "Pepper and Ollie are still upstairs, are they?"

Azalea's eyes opened wide, and she nodded. I raised my eyebrow.

"Fortuna, we should definitely go see what they've found."

Before I could reply, Martin walked past Azalea and into the back. Once we heard his heavy steps heading to the second floor, Azalea looked at me and whispered, "He knows that I know you're not just spending time together, right?"

"Honestly, I have no idea what he knows," I told her. "But if you want to work extra hours this week, I've got you covered, and you'll really be helping me out."

"Did you find anything out about the vase at Martin's house?" she whispered.

"Not really." I shook my head. "One thing I *did* notice, though. I don't think Martin's employees at his home are *nearly* as loyal as he thinks they are."

"Oh?"

"Yeah, it wasn't really any one thing," I told her as I hung up my keys and walked past her. "Just a feeling watching them interact with him."

Azalea nodded and then cocked her head. "Did you say anything to him?"

"Who, Martin?"

She nodded again.

"Not yet," I told her as I patted her on the shoulder. "We had a bit of a tense discussion at his house. I decided to wait until I was back here to bring it up. Might help to have Pepper and Ollie around to defuse any tension."

"You think Pepper would *defuse* tension?"

I laughed. "I'm about to go find out."

* * *

I closed the door to the front of the studio and headed up to join the rest in my second floor living area. The stairway was bathed pale sunlight as the afternoon faded into dusk. It still held a slightly musty smell despite my near constant cleaning. A remnant of the twenty years the building had been Spike's tomb. But it was quiet. An in-between moment of peace.

"How *dare* you!" Martin shouted from above. Oh boy.

"You *knew* we were going to be looking into footage from your house, idiot!" Pepper's acerbic voice whipped back in response. "Did you not realize an investigation would involve, you know, *investigating?*"

I stopped on the stairs and sighed.

"I *don't* want her to know about that!" Martin shot back.

My ears perked up. He doesn't want me to know about what?

"You *promised* me that you would respect the bro code," Martin said fiercely.

"Dude, I *didn't* look in your bedroom, I swear," Ollie responded calmly, his voice woven through with amusement. "But if you want me to cut out all these women running around the first floor of your house? I'm not going to have much footage left to go through."

"Besides, it's kind of *easy* to tell what happened," Pepper pointed out. "How many options *are* there for scantily dressed women once they go up the stairs with you? Did we miss a game room on the second floor?" Pepper paused, and I listened for Martin's response, but she continued. "I don't *need* to look at the footage from your bedroom to put two and two together, Romeo."

I took a deep breath and finished ascending the stairs.

"Has anyone thought about ordering in dinner?" I asked to announce my presence and try to defuse the tension. The three turned to stare at me, emerging from the stairway alcove. "I can tell you that I *definitely* do not have enough food to feed four people."

"I can have one of my employees bring us dinner from the complex," Martin said, pulling out his cell phone. "Does anyone have a preference?"

"I don't care." I shrugged.

"Well, let's *definitely* skip the Centre, right?" Pepper was staring at Martin, her eyes filled with fury. Martin looked like a deer in the headlights, his eyes moving back and forth between Pepper and me.

"Whatever you want is fine, Martin." I

shrugged. "It would be helpful, thanks. Like I said, I don't care."

Pepper whirled on me. "You would if you—"

"I wouldn't," I told her. "And I'm not just talking about where to order dinner from. I don't care *what* women were in his house. There's never been a moment, not a *single second*, that Martin and I were committed exclusively to one another. I don't *care* who was in his house. I don't *care* who went up the stairs. I don't care." The cold pronouncement dropped on the room like a guillotine slicing off everyone's fury and indignation.

"Well, *that's* good," Ollie smiled, gesturing toward his computer. "Because there's a lot of 'em."

"Including *Evangeline Laroux*." Pepper spat the name like it was a curse.

"Well, if that's the case," I said, shrugging. "Maybe she *wasn't* so unjustified in coming over here after all."

Pepper continued to seethe. "You know, if he—"

"Can I talk to you?"

The last question had come from Martin, and it crossed my mind to simply ignore that he'd asked it. Pepper's face grew even redder, thanks to his cutting her off. It felt like time stopped for a moment. Martin, angry and concerned. Pepper enraged. Ollie—

Well, Ollie kind of looked like he was watching an episode of *The Real Housewives of Mystic's End*. There didn't *seem* to be much that could flap the unflappable Ollie Kane.

"Fortuna?" Martin prodded. I stared at him.

Why was I still *bothering* with this guy? He clearly had so many things to hide, a life I knew nothing about, and more secrets than I could shake a wand at. On top of all *that*, he ran a greyhound racetrack—something that I couldn't stand. Just because Martin Salvi was handsome and sexy and charming *didn't* mean he wasn't dangerous.

A cobra was *stunningly* beautiful, sleek, and moved with incredible grace.

Didn't mean I wanted to cuddle up in bed with it.

"I'm standing right here, Martin." I held up my hands. "Say anything you have to say. We're all friends here, right?"

Martin glanced at Pepper. His expression conveyed he *wasn't* sure we were all friends here. Not even remotely.

"Look, I never said I wasn't dating other people."

"Martin, I never *asked* you not to date other people, and I never asked if you were dating other people. Your life is your own business. You made it clear you felt that way, as well, when you stopped talking to me. I don't see what the problem is here."

Martin stiffened. His eyes flickered with surprise, and the corners crinkled. They bore into me, searching my expression as if looking for something missing, something beyond my statement. Something he wanted to see but didn't.

Then it hit me.

Holy cow.

He *wanted* me to care. He wanted me to care that Ollie and Pepper had spotted women coming in and out of his mansion with some regularity. He *wanted* me to be jealous. He *wanted* me to feel the same jealousy *he* felt for Gabe.

My eyes narrowed.

Was this all another put-on? Was this just some high-tech manipulation designed to make me jealous? Ollie clearly outlined what footage he would be putting together. Despite their back and forth about some bro code, Martin had known that Pepper wouldn't be able to keep silent about what she saw.

The more I got to know Martin Salvi, the less I trusted him.

"She may not care, but buddy, you have a lot of nerve leaving dinner with Fortuna and then picking up some floozy at the track. Repeatedly," Pepper said, pausing again for his response. When he had none, she asked, "How did you not think this would come out? You asked us to look into this for you. We told you what we were doing—"

Martin's frowned deepened. "I didn't ask *you* to get involved in this at all. Let's be clear about *that*."

"Boy, it *really* burns your britches when you can't control everything, doesn't it?"

"Okay, everyone, let's take it down a notch." Pepper knew better than to engage directly with Martin on this kind of thing. "Martin doesn't need to explain his personal life to us for us to investigate the women that were in his house."

Pepper looked at me and gritted her teeth.

"Ollie, you and Martin go through the list and see if you can spot anyone with a grudge, that's acting suspicious. I'm going to assume you didn't find any footage of someone *obviously* exchanging out one urn for another?"

Ollie shook his head. "Not *obviously*, no. There's footage of the butler—Jerome?" Martin nodded. "Jerome taking it off the pedestal to dust it. Another evening, three or so people gathered around it, but I don't know who they are. Laroux spent a lot of time looking at it. Other than that, it hadn't moved, and I didn't find anyone *particularly* interested in it beyond that."

"Okay, let's identify and concentrate on those

people, then." I turned to Pepper. "How about you and I go downstairs and have a chat?"

Pepper looked like she wanted to argue with me, but then she shrugged and stomped toward the stairs. "If you want to talk, we'll *talk*. But don't think I'll hold my tongue."

"I would never," I breathed as I followed. Ollie chuckled.

Martin did not.

* * *

"That man had so many women in and out of his house that you would have thought he ran a free makeup counter in his bedroom!" Pepper's eyes flashed with fiery indignation as her rage flamed on my behalf. "How can you not care that the guy you thought about *dating* is some philandering jerk!"

"Pepper, we never got in a committed relationship—"

"Thank goodness! The guy's in a relationship with half the women in the state of Arkansas!"

I rubbed my eyes. Pepper could be...taxing.

And I didn't know how to *explain* it to Pepper. Maybe months ago, when I first arrived in Mystic's End, this news would have hurt me. Back when I had a few more stars in my eyes where Martin was concerned. His disappearance to "protect" me had dampened *much* of the attraction I felt for him. He was handsome, yes. And he and I shared a similar past—at least *if* I could believe him.

But he'd abandoned me. So I had become much more cautious about trusting him.

And with all I'd learned about him, this wasn't really a surprise.

"This is nothing more than a piece of information. I appreciate you guys uncovering it because, frankly, it's good to know," I admitted. "But finding out Martin isn't precisely who I thought he was doesn't really hurt me. If anything, it confirms for me that my decisions to keep him at arm's length were *probably* good ones."

"Oh, man, Gabe is going to blow his *stack* when he hears about this—"

I frowned. "You *do* realize that you're slut-shaming Martin, Ms. Feminist."

"I am *not*. You can't slut-shame a man. They *have* no shame."

I rolled my eyes. "Just because it rarely happens to men doesn't mean it *can't* happen to them," I pointed out, lowering my voice so Azalea didn't overhear. "You're passing judgment on Martin because he's a sexually active adult male with a lot of romantic partners. How do you *not* see that as slut-shaming? What Martin does in his bedroom is his own business. It doesn't affect me."

"It would if you were one of the people *in* his bedroom!"

"But I'm not, right? So it doesn't."

Pepper blew out an exasperated breath. "Do you *practice* being the voice of reason, or is it something that just comes naturally to you?" She leveled a stare at me. "It's annoying sometimes."

I laughed. "Look, I'm glad that we found the information. Even more so for the fact that Martin *clearly* didn't want me to know about it. I'm less concerned about the parade of women than about the fact that he clearly intended to keep his...*other* life hidden."

"One *more* thing he's hiding," Pepper grumbled.

"Right. All I'm saying is lay off him, huh? This doesn't bother me. Well," I paused and frowned. "The parade of women doesn't bother me. That he may have been *seeing* Evangeline Laroux bothers me a bit. She *really* thinks she's in love with him. My question now is whether he did anything to stoke those feelings in her."

"You can't *make* someone fall in love with you."

"No, but you can be honest with them about where a casual relationship will lead and where it won't. Is he?" I asked Pepper. "Or is he toying with her, making her *think* there's a future when there isn't?"

"Are you actually concerned about the feelings of that miserable drunken—"

"Manners," I said absently.

"Yeah, I don't really have them," she responded. Suddenly, her eyes widened. "Oh! By the way— what do we know about Jeeves?"

"I know his name is Chris something, but hardly anything. Why?"

"There was something weird in the footage we looked at." Pepper turned her head away and gazed up toward the second floor. "At least, it was to me."

"Oh?"

"Jeeves wasn't on *any* of it. Not in the house, not *outside* the house. Even when they pulled up in the limo. I never could spot him getting in *or* out of the car. It was like he wasn't even there. Since he's usually stuck up Martin's butt, it just seemed strange."

I frowned. That was strange. "That doesn't make sense."

"We should ask Martin—"

"Let's not mention this to Martin."

A raised eyebrow. "What happened to not wanting to hide things from him?"

"Clearly, he operates by a set of rules that allow him to hide things from me," I told her, turning toward the stairwell. "Maybe it's time I start following his rules."

NINE

"The three women—"

"Three *women*, Fortuna. There were three *women*," Pepper said, clearly ignoring everything I said downstairs about not poking Martin. She said the word *women* with such derision I half-expected a women's rights group to walk in and slap her.

"Like I said," Ollie continued, chuckling. "These three women?" Ollie turned the computer screen toward me. Despite Pepper's implication that the gaggle of floozies surrounding Martin's urn was some kind of artistic prelude to a sleazy foursome? All three appeared to be just a year or two away from getting rooms in Wrinkle City.

"They're members of the Grace Gang. It's a women's group from Holy Grove Church."

I frowned. "What's a *Grace Gang?*"

"Haven't you ever been to a church?" Pepper asked, incredulous.

"I went to Spike's funeral. And Mr. Maddox's. Beyond that? Not really."

"Churches have lots of little groups that do different things." Pepper sat down on a chair and splayed out, her chin on her hand. "The women's group is just that, a group for the women in the congregation. *Officially*, the Grace Gang is supposed to help women express their godly femininity—" Pepper rolled her eyes "—by serving others. Bake sales, raising money for the needy. That sort of thing."

"That sounds harmless. And unofficially?"

"It's hard to turn down three sweet grandmas haranguing you to go to church. The more money you have to donate? The harder they harangue."

The bathroom door opened, and Martin rejoined the group. His annoyance at how the investigation had gone sparked around him like an unspoken indictment. "They come by once a month to bring baked goods and harass me to join Kane's church. I let them in for the baked goods. Well, that, and because I want to keep a good relationship with Dexter Kane."

"Why do you think those women were so interested in the urn?" I asked him.

"If I *remember* correctly, they were upset that I had it." Martin's gaze drifted upward as he concentrated. "They didn't get too confrontational about it, but one of them knew what it was. They said it was a relic of a satanic belief system, and that having it on display invited Satan in my home."

"That sounds like a reason to steal it," Pepper pointed out. "I mean, if you thought you were *literally* removing Satan from a house, wouldn't *you* want to steal it?"

"But to make a replica of it and *switch* it out?" I crossed my arms. "I find it hard to believe three little old ladies from the church would go through all that trouble to save your soul, Martin. No offense."

"None taken," he said smoothly. Martin's face relaxed back into his usual nonchalance— nonchalance that I'd now come to suspect was a practiced mask he could put on and take off at will. "If I remember correctly, though, none of those women had anything large enough to hide something that size. Was there anything on the video that indicated they *might* have done it?"

"There were a few minutes where I really couldn't track what was going on," Ollie admitted as he punched up a section of the video. "Here.

They're tightly gathered. The angle of the camera doesn't give me much of an ability to see what's going on in the center. But I also didn't see any movement that might indicate they're filching an old pot, either."

"So, we should talk to the old women at the church—"

"That will *not* be me." Pepper glared at me.

"It's my dad's church, so I can drop by and talk to them," Ollie volunteered.

"Oh, right," Pepper said, and then chewed on her fingernail. "I almost forgot your dad is Dexter Kane." Her eyes clouded, and I could practically feel her attraction to Ollie deflate like a balloon. "So, you still talk to your dad, huh?"

"He *is* my dad." Ollie looked at her pointedly. "We don't get to choose family."

We can reject them, though.

"This is a strange crew," Martin said as he glanced around. "Parents that cast long shadows. I wonder what the odds are?"

"My parents don't cast a long shadow," Pepper told him. "My mom and dad have been happily married for a gazillion years now, and they are genuinely good people. Unlike—" Pepper abruptly stopped herself and looked around as if she just realized who she was talking to. "Yeah, um, sorry about that. My mouth runs away from my brain sometimes."

"It's part of your charm," Ollie told her affectionately, and she blushed.

"You're *such* a nice boy," Pepper responded. "Hard to believe you're Dexter Kane's son."

He shut the laptop and stood up, stretching. "Look, I have absolutely no illusions about who my father is. I have a relationship with him that makes the accommodations I need to make to be able to maintain some semblance of a connection with him. I imagine Martin here has had to do the same." Ollie hitched his head in Martin's direction. "For now, it works. That may not always be the case, and I realize that."

"We all do the best we can," Martin added.

"You guys never talk about your mothers," I asked suddenly, curious. "Do you have relationships with them?"

A flash of pain exploded in the room, and I felt it like a gut punch to the solar plexus. It happened so quickly and so forcefully I couldn't track where it came from. Glancing around, I realized it didn't have just *one* origin. Both Martin and Ollie's faces held shadow webs of remembered misery.

"My mom's no longer with us," Ollie told me quietly.

"Mine, either," Martin added.

That's such a coincidence. Mary, Gabe's Mom, and Martin, and—

Pepper and I glanced at one another.

She was thinking what I was thinking, and I didn't need psychic intuition to know that. *What are the chances that the three men closest to us—no, four, if you count Spike's ghost—all lost their mothers so young?* The chances of that *had* to be astronomical.

"I'm so sorry," Pepper said. Looking at Martin, she added, "Really, I am. For both of you."

"It happened a long time ago," he shrugged. "I hardly think about it anymore."

Without a doubt, I knew he was lying.

* * *

"I'm *not* riding on that."

"It'll be fine." Ollie held out a helmet toward me, and I shook my head.

"I'm not riding on a motorcycle. I'll throw up the dinner we just ate. *All* over you."

"You *teleported* to an alternate universe with the circus, but you won't ride on the back of my bike?" He slipped his head into the helmet and flipped up the visor. "The two helmets are connected so you can talk to me if there's an issue. I promise I'll take it easy."

I heard Gideon whine through the front window. Then an image of a greyhound in a helmet perched atop a speeding motorcycle like he was *Easy Rider* flashed in my mind. "I got news for you, dog, if you could take notes of what you saw at the church, I'd let *you* do this instead," I called over my shoulder. "I *have* a van, why can't you just leave your bike here? I'll drive. The van. Safely."

"Yeah, *that's* not gonna happen." Ollie shrugged. "She goes where I go. Come on, I'll be a captive audience. You can tell me all the reasons I should date your best friend."

"Right, like I'm going to want you around *more* after this."

I stared at the motorcycle with apprehension as Ollie laughed. Finally, I accepted the outstretched helmet and slipped it on my head. My hands shaking, I climbed up behind him. The bike roared and rumbled to life as I buried my head in my hands.

Which is hard to do when you're wearing a motorcycle helmet.

"You going to have to put your arms around my waist and hold on." Ollie's voice buzzed in my ear. "You don't want to fall off, do you?"

"Oh, man, why did you have to say that?" I whispered as I wrapped my arms around his lithe, muscular body.

"These are really great microphones." Ollie chuckled as his posture slightly changed. "Even if you whisper, I can hear you. And I said that because it got you to hold on," he told me as my stomach jumped. "Are you ready?"

"No, I'm not—" My denial of reality was cut off by a scream as the motorbike jerked to life.

I took a second to realize the scream was mine.

"Can you stop screaming?" Ollie asked calmly as the wind whipped against me. "Like I said, these microphones are pretty sensitive. You can just curse me at a normal decibel level, and it *will* get the point across. The screaming's a *little* distracting."

"I'm sorry. I'm sorry. But I don't curse," I whispered, my eyes scrunched tight. "I was brought up not to curse. So I don't curse. But oh my gosh, I've never wanted to curse much in my life—"

"Ooh, come on, you're not enjoying this even a little bit? Look at the scenery."

"I haven't opened my eyes since we pulled away from the curb."

"You haven't?"

"No. No. I have *not*," I said as the bike lurched to the right, and I held on tighter. "Oh my stars, are we crashing? We're *crashing*, aren't we!" My stomach lurched the other direction.

"That was just a turn," Ollie chuckled. "We're on the road leading to Holy Grove. Beautiful scenery. You might enjoy it if you decide to open your eyes."

With much trepidation, I opened my eyes. Darkness and green whizzed past at a rate that seemed supernatural at best, *catastrophically* dangerous at worst. Lit street lights created a strobe effect as we blew by them.

There were few cars or trucks on the road this time of night. Holy Grove's location was on the direct opposite end of town from Mystic's End's Complex (of expensive sin). If there were roads heavy with traffic, they were the roads leading to strip clubs, fancy restaurants, greyhound racing, and disco clubs. Not churches.

Martin's entertainment complex did *not* need to send out little old lady pressure brigades. The mere existence of the place drew in people and their money daily.

Ollie took a sharp left, and the bike jumped.

"What was that?" I screamed, clutching tighter.

"We're here," he answered. "Was just a little bump at the bottom of the drive. Relax, you made it here in one piece." Ollie coasted the bike to a stop, and I practically launched myself toward the asphalt with an ungainly tumble. I heard the helmet slam against the curb. "Jeez, Fortuna, are you all right?"

"I don't like you anymore," I told him as I

scrambled to sit up and yanked the hot helmet off. "That was the worst experience I've ever had in my life."

"Really? The *worst*?"

"Fine, maybe I'm exaggerating. *Maybe*." I stood up and handed him the helmet.

"You want to drive back? Maybe you can do better." Ollie smirked as he attached the helmets to the bike. "I'd let you drive my bike." He grinned at me. "It's insured."

"Stop talking about it. I *don't* want to think about it." I glared at the evil death machine. My limbs felt like they were still vibrating.

"So, let me do the talking with Dad, okay?" Ollie said, walking toward the double doors. Then he stopped, paused, and turned. "Remember, the plan we're telling him about why we're here, and you're a woman, anyway, so best to let me do the talking, right?"

"Wait a minute. What does *that* mean?"

Ollie smirked and walked away.

* * *

We all thought Ollie and me visiting Dexter Kane's church was the best idea for a few reasons.

Martin had a business relationship with Kane it

was vital for him to maintain. And Pepper...Well, let's just say Pepper had done a few stories about Holy Grove Church, and they weren't stories that the Reverend Kane was all that pleased with. Pepper likely could not talk to the women without arousing suspicion.

I, on the other hand, was relatively new to Mystic's End. It was plausible that I would be interested in finding a church. It *wasn't* likely that I would be interested in Dexter Kane's church, but *he* didn't know that.

"Hey, Dad," Ollie called warmly as we entered the chapel. "I thought I'd find you here."

"Good evening, son," the sketchy preacher called back. "What brings you out to the edge of town?" Dexter frowned. "Something wrong?"

"Nothing like that. I think you know my friend Fortuna, right?"

"Of course, I am *well* acquainted with her, son." Dexter smiled to imply a relationship much closer than he and I had ever had. His expression made me feel like I needed a shower. "How's that dog I sold you? I'd ask you if he was worth the price you paid, but to be honest? Even if you'd *raced* him, he likely wouldn't have been."

I resisted the urge to kick the preacher in the shins.

"Gideon's doing fine, sir." I nodded respectfully.

"You kept the name, did you?" Kane looked surprised. "I wouldn't have thought a woman like you—" he gestured up and down as if the type he spoke of was obvious—"would've kept such a holy name. Something like Demon or Baphomet would be more your speed, perhaps?"

My urge to kick the Reverend was traveling a little higher on his body.

"Dad, there's *no* need for you to make comments like that. Fortuna is thinking about joining the church." Ollie flung his arm around my shoulder, and I smiled despite my clenched teeth. "She was asking me about the women's group. Are any of the ladies from the Grace Gang here? I'd love to introduce her."

"*Her?*" Kane asked, shocked. "*She* wants to join a *church?*"

"Well, the more sinful the person, the better the get for you, right?" Ollie squeezed me.

I *had* two feet. I could kick two people at once.

TEN

"Allow me to introduce you to Tula Jenkins, Beulah Conroe, *and* Tallulah Abernathy," Reverend Kane boomed as we walked into a small room off the chapel. He extended his arm and escorted me toward three older women seated on the other side of the room. Gray and silver hair vibrated as they knitted with intent concentration using identical colors of yarn. "That's Beulah in the center, as usual. These three women are the *backbone* of the Grace Gang. And that's no brag, Miss Delphi."

Beulah jerked her head up and stared as if surprised by our presence. "Delphi?" she shouted. The two other women flanking her cast their eyes hesitantly toward me. "Reverend, did you just say *that* girl is a *Delphi*? And you brought her in here?"

"The only one we have in town, Beulah." Dexter Kane nodded. "It may be hard for you to believe, but my son has brought us a lost...well, not a *sheep*, clearly. A wandering wolf, perhaps? Looking to find a new pack?"

"We *shoot* wolves in these here parts," Beulah said ominously.

Friendly bunch.

Had I tried to imagine the women of the Witches' Council as elderly, this is *probably* what I would've imagined.

"I didn't know there were wolves in Arkansas, ma'am," I answered politely.

"We used to have red wolves," Tula answered quietly. Tallulah glared at her, and she dropped her head demurely, her cheeks pinking slightly.

"Yeah, they *ain't* here no more," Beulah barked. "Probably because we shot 'em all. Weren't any more Delphis till *you* showed up, neither."

I froze. "Any *more*?"

"You got cotton in your ears, girl?" the old woman asked me. Her tone was nasty.

"Now, Beulah, is that any way to treat someone thinking about coming to worship with us?" Reverend Kane asked the cantankerous crone. His voice held an unmistakable tone of admonishment.

She snorted at the pastor and rolled her eyes. "Beulah, I need you to turn on some of that charm and convince Fortuna here that she should attend church Sunday."

"I'm surprised she hasn't been struck by lightning yet just walking in the place," Beulah murmured, snorting again. "All the Delphis are *nothing* but trouble. Nothing but trouble, I tell you."

"There aren't that many left, Beulah," Tallulah Abernathy patted her friend on the knee. "Most people don't remember 'em, anyway."

"Trouble, trouble," Beulah murmured, her eyes narrowing.

What did she mean, *all* the Delphis? My name wasn't given. It was a name I *chose* after joining the Langdon circus. I looked around for Ollie, but he hadn't followed us into this room.

"That's *just* an old wives tale, Beulah May," Reverend Kane told the woman dismissively. "You ladies and your stories. Now, can I leave Miss Delphi here with you to work your magic on her?"

My eyes narrowed at his statement, and without conscious thought, I reached into my memory for the shields Gunther once taught me to use. One by one by one, I threw up fences and walls and protective shells around myself. *Just* in case Kane's statement wasn't a quaint turn of phrase.

"We will do our best, pastor," Beulah told him, smiling cynically. "You know we *always* do.

"I'll be outside with my son," Dexter Kane nodded.

He spun on his heel and whistled cheerfully as he walked out the door.

* * *

Tula and Tallulah sat at Beulah's right and left hands, their eyes back down, knitting tools and yarn in their lap. I wondered for a split second just how effective an auric shell would be against a straight needle coming at me wielded by an eighty-year-old.

"So, Ollie and Martin have told me a bit about your church—"

"Martin who?" Tallulah asked sharply.

"Martin Salvi." I smiled through the tension in the room. "He mentioned the three of you stop by once a month or so. He absolutely loves your visits," I lied.

"Well, *now* I understand why the Reverend brought you in here." Beulah nodded, her face melting into understanding. "I would've thought a woman like *you* would be as welcome in *this* church as a skunk at a backyard barbecue, but ol' Dexter *has* been chomping at the bit to get Martin in the flock. I guess he means to do it through you, seems like."

"Is *this* normally how you persuade people to join up?" I asked.

"We *don't* normally persuade *women* to join up," Tallulah pointed out.

"She's right," Tula agreed. Her tone was more friendly than the others, but still cautious. "Our congregation is very traditional, Miss Delphi. Women can't typically join without their husbands, you see."

"You don't allow single women to join your church?" I asked, shocked.

"We believe women need a *man* to make those decisions for them," Beulah nodded. "At least, that's what Reverend Kane says. And we follow what Reverend Kane says."

I had realized that Reverend Kane was conservative, but *this* was a conservatism beyond anything I had expected. Granted, I wasn't *that* familiar with churches—my adoptive parents had never been religious that I could tell. But I'd never heard of a church that literally *barred* women from joining on their own. I mean, who does that?

"What denomination is this church?" I asked.

"We make our *own* rules," Beulah answered.

"Well, the *pastor* makes the rules, Beulah," Tula corrected politely. The old woman was the smallest of the three, tiny in stature with shining silver hair and kind eyes. She turned and smiled. "We're unaffiliated with any particular church, religion, or doctrine that *you* might know of, Fortuna. May I call you Fortuna?" I nodded. "We're distinctly Mystic's End, you see. There's no other church like us."

"I still don't think I understand—"

"Then *join*," Beulah barked. "You'll understand then. Should I get the book?"

"The book?"

"That you sign. To *join*," she responded impatiently.

"I don't think so, not quite yet," I answered. "I'd have to talk to Martin about it before signing anything, of course." I was incredibly impressed with myself that I got *that* line out without throwing up a little bit in my mouth. "So, you're not Catholic or Evangelical or—"

"We are the *Holy Grove* Church, Miss Delphi. I *told* you. That's *all* you need to know. You're called, or you're not. Since the pastor brought you in here, *clearly,* you've been called."

I frowned in confusion. "Called by who?"

"Reverend Kane, obviously," Beulah said with exasperation.

"And is *this* the holy grove?" I asked as I gestured to a grove of trees out the window.

"We don't *talk* about the grove with *outsiders*," Tallulah said fiercely.

I peeked out the window again to make sure the foliage I saw *wasn't* a cornfield. Because I have to admit, I was wondering if I'd accidentally walked into a Stephen King novel.

"I understand." I nodded respectfully. "I meant no disrespect by asking. I am curious about something you said earlier, though—who are the Delphis?"

"You sound like that Pepper Stanford with all your—hey, *wait* a minute." Beulah's eyes narrowed as she pushed herself swiftly from her chair. "Aren't you friends with that wretch of a girl?" When I walked in, she seemed surprised that "a Delphi" even existed in Mystic's End.

Now she knew who I hung out with?

"Martin and I both are, yes." I nodded, smiling sweetly and tilting my head. "Conroe...are you Detective Beau Conroe's mother?" I asked, recalling the blonde detective I first met at the police station months ago. Beulah nodded. "And you, Abernathy...any relation to Jeff or Hoyt?"

"Hoyt's my son," Tallulah answered slowly. "And Jeff's my grandson."

Okay, maybe it shouldn't surprise me that Beulah wasn't familiar with me—Detective Conroe and I were not close. But *Tallulah?* I nearly sent her grandson to *prison* for the accidental death of Spike, my roommate. Plus the fact that her son was furious at me for buying Gideon and then removing him from their kennel, costing the family thousands of dollars.

How did she *not* know who I was?

"Your son's construction company built the Mystic's End Racetrack," I said, nodding. "Why do you think *he* wasn't able to get Martin to join the church? I would've thought that Jeff and Martin work together quite a bit, between the construction work and the fact that your family owns a greyhound racing kennel."

"*Don't* answer that, Tallulah," Beulah snapped.

"Okay." She nodded and then tilted her head, a confused look on her face. "Why not?"

"What are you *really* here for, little girl?" Beulah crossed her arms and leaned forward menacingly. Despite her attempts to cut me down to the size of a child by repeatedly calling me a *girl*, I *was* bigger and stronger than the slight old woman.

And yet...*something* told me to be cautious about toying with her.

"Did you steal anything from Martin Salvi?" I asked point blank.

The three women looked horrified at the accusation.

"Reverend Kane would *never* forgive us if we stole from his prime—" Tallulah choked as Beulah whacked her, hard, in the stomach with a bony fist. The old woman doubled-over under the assault and the daggered stare, while coughing like her lungs were about to come up.

Beulah looked up at me, ignoring the doubled-over woman beside her. "No. We did not and *would* not. And I am offended that *you* would even suggest such a thing. You," she sneered. "You of all people? Accuse *us*? *Please*."

I cut my eyes to Tallulah and then back to Beulah. "What's that supposed to mean?"

"Miss Delphi," Tula said, stepping in front of the angry Beulah. "We are good, pious women. We practice our beliefs faithfully, and one of our beliefs is that we never steal from anyone. Not ever. It's a sin, and we would never do it."

"Your beliefs don't include not punching your friends in the gut, I take it?"

"Beulah struggles with her prayerful observances, it's true." Tula nodded, casting a sympathetic look in the angry Beulah's direction. "But I *assure* you, all of us have only been in Mr. Salvi's home together, and I would never countenance a theft from one like...him."

I didn't *say* something was stolen from Martin's home. "What does that mean, one *like him*?"

"He's under the protection of the *blood devil*, child," Tallulah snapped. "We're not idiots!"

"Tallulah, you talk too much!" Beulah shouted. "You!" She whirled toward me. "You need to leave! You are an *earth devil,* and you're making Tallulah forget herself! Go! There's no place for you here, demon!"

Well, *that* was clear enough.

"Please, forgive them," Tula told me as she stepped closer. "We are simple women, and we are easily upset. Even if you *are* demonic, I don't sense you are *entirely* black-hearted." She smiled kindly. "If you only came to find out if we stole from Martin, you have done your duty to your man—"

"He's not my—"

"—as I assure you, we did not. Go in peace." Tula nodded as if she was bestowing a benediction. "I hope you find what you're looking for."

"Earth devil!" Beulah shouted again as I made a beeline for the door.

* * *

Dexter Kane could barely hide his disappointment I had not "signed my name to the book," but he let us go with no further pressure.

"Mechanical devil," I muttered at the motorcycle as Ollie held out the helmet.

"What did you say?" he smirked as I climbed on.

"What's a blood devil?" My stomach lurched as he pulled away from the church and drove slowly around the parking lot toward the exit. "And an earth devil?"

"A vampire, and a witch," Ollie said in my ear as the wind whipped around me again. "Did the Grace Gang talk to you about the different devils? That's kind of surprising. Not something they'd usually open with."

"There's more?"

"Ghosts? Spirit devils. Shapeshifters? Fauna Devils. Nymphs? Flora devils."

"If you were raised in *that* church, how on earth did you wind up at Avalon Grove in Mickwac?" I asked him, referencing Priestess Goodfellow's magic shop and coven back in Texas. "Those women did everything *but* throw holy water on me."

"There's no holy water because, obviously, it's got devils in it," Ollie responded with a small chuckle. "Dad's not a Christian, though I don't know that some of the folks that go to the church understand that. Well, the people really into it do. Anyway, as I grew up, I never totally bought into his worldview. And when I got to college, I wanted to know what all the devils were and why Dad was so obsessed with them."

"No offense, Ollie, but those women? They sounded more like members of a cult than members of a church."

"There's a finer line between those things than you might think," he answered. "Did you find out anything about the urn?"

"I don't think they took it. I mean, I think they would be capable, but they seemed really...I don't know, in awe of Martin?" I felt Ollie's head nod yes. "By the way, do you know of anyone in town that has the last name I do?"

"Addington?"

"Delphi."

"I thought that was your magical name."

"It is," I admitted. "But the Grace Gang said some things that implied there used to be other people in this town with the same name."

"I don't, but to be honest, I've never been super into this town's weird history. You know, it may be time to talk to Miss Bessie," Ollie said. "I bet *she'd* know. By the way, hold on."

The engine roared as we sped up, and I stopped being capable of talking through my panic.

But I didn't scream.

So, improvement.

ELEVEN

"She said *what* now?" Pepper asked, her voice sharp with disbelief.

We stood in the bedroom on the third floor of my building, far from the stairway (to ensure no one down below could overhear us). Martin and Ollie remained on the second floor finishing their identification of the women from the security footage. Jeeves, as always, stayed with them. Azalea had left before we arrived back since the store had now closed for the day.

"Are you telling me you've never heard about these devils? Blood devils and earth devils and, I don't know, water devils, whipped cream devils?" I asked her while moving toward the bed to scratch Gideon's exposed belly. "Or this grove? You've lived here all your life, and they seemed pretty...well, okay, not *open* about it, but it certainly slipped out quickly enough. And it seemed pretty important to their world view."

"I thought you went over there to investigate the urn?"

"I did."

"How on earth did all this gibberish come up?"

"*Gibberish?*" I asked, stiffening. "This isn't *gibberish*, Pepper. That church knows about paranormals," I told her. "The fact that they call them something different doesn't change the fact that they're talking about supernatural people. Vampires, witches—they seem to know about all of them."

"So?" Pepper looked confused. "What does any of this have to do with the urn?"

"Did you hit your *head* while I was gone? Have you been listening to *anything* I just said?" I asked her archly. "I'm not talking about the stupid urn right now!"

"You know, *you've* been the one telling me not to go off half-cocked every time I pass a rabbit hole, Fortuna. I'm trying to stay focused."

"*Now* you're taking my advice?" I asked Pepper acidly.

Pepper looked surprised at my tone. "What on earth has got *you* all discombobulated? You took

Miss Bessie slapping you with a shrug and rolled your eyes at a magic book being chucked at you by a spontaneous hole in the ground. A church knowing about paranormals has you freaked? *Really?* Why's this making you all...*me*-like?"

"Oh, I don't know." I sighed and dropped down on the bed next to Gideon. He raised his head, his soft eyes gazing at my face. Then he yawned, lowered his head, and went back to sleep. "Actually, that's not true. I *do* know. Beulah Conroe mentioned something about disliking *the Delphis*. As if there was a family with that name in this town."

Pepper frowned. "I thought you chose that name when you join the circus?"

"I did. Hence my discombobulation. At least, I figure that's what's got me out of sorts." I squinted over at the magical book the grove in the woods had given me...

The *grove*.

"That couldn't *possibly* be the *holy grove* they're talking about," I whispered, scrambling off the bed. I peered down at the sealed book, closed to me unless I opened it while Miss Bessie was nearby. "They were *so* defensive over the grove. Wouldn't answer what it was, said they don't talk to *outsiders* about it."

"You think Kane's church has something to do with the place we found the book?"

"How did you know where to go?" I asked her as I picked up the leather-bound tome and examined its cover. It was dull, nondescript. There was nothing about it that indicated the book was magical or even unusual. It could have been a fancy photo album picked up from a craft store. Well, an *old* photo album.

"Irma at the library. I told you, I found descriptions in *The Witch History of Mystic,* got a map, and figured out where I *thought* they were talking about." Pepper shrugged. "We go there, the earth shakes, the ground spits out an altar with a book on it when you ask, you take it, we leave." Pepper left out the part about us tripping over a dead body on the way out, but I suppose from the book hunt perspective, it wasn't essential to the point.

"That path led directly to that grove," I mused as we both gazed at the book. "And then it just stopped. As if people had walked out there before lots of times. You don't think *that's* the holy grove the church women were talking about, do you?"

"You think Reverend Kane's church is about *that* book?"

"I don't know." I shrugged. "Like I said, they

were awfully interested in all manner of devils.
Why not a devil book?"

"You've certainly made Mystic's End a lot more
interesting, Fortuna, I'll give you that," Pepper
muttered, staring at the book and chewed her lower
lip. "Honestly, the best person to ask about Dexter
Kane's church would be Ollie. He grew up in it. He
must know all their secrets."

"Has he ever told any of this to you?" Pepper
shook her head no. "He's still loyal to his dad, you
know. I could see the affection the two of them had
for one another. I don't know that Ollie will be so
willing to betray his father's secrets."

"You know, there's still *one* other option,"
Pepper pointed out.

"Miss Bessie," we said simultaneously. Gideon
barked as if in agreement.

* * *

"Hey, everything okay?" Ollie asked, concerned,
as we came down the stairs.

"I'm good," Pepper answered brightly. Ollie
glanced over at me. "Oh, you meant *her*. She's fine."
Ollie smiled at Pepper, and she stuck her tongue
out at him.

"Ollie mentioned you don't think the church

ladies had anything to do with the urn disappearing?" Martin asked me. Pepper walked over behind Ollie and glanced at his computer screen.

"Yeah, I don't know if I'd *completely* take them off the suspect list? I mean, there *could* be something going on that I didn't pick up on. The conversation was...weird. But I got the feeling from talking to them that the theft of antiquity from *you* wasn't something they'd be willing to do."

"So, you think they'd steal, but just not from *me*?" Martin's voice was startled. Jeeves and Martin glanced at one another warily. "Did they actually say that?"

"More or less. That surprises you?"

"I just can't think of any reason why *I* would be so special," Martin said, casting another sidelong glance at Jeeves. Jeeves remained, as usual, impassive and motionless except for his eyes.

His eyes were cold.

I stared at the guard, trying to pinpoint what about him made me feel so unsettled. It wasn't just his silence or his stance. It wasn't just that the man never seemed to sleep. There was an aura around him that screamed he was dangerous. But I just couldn't put my finger on it...

There was something...something...

He's under the protection of the blood devil, child. We're not idiots!

What's a blood devil?

A vampire.

I gasped.

"What?" Pepper stood up fast, staring at me. "What's wrong?"

Jeeves and I stared at one another across the room.

"How did I *not* figure this out?" I whispered. "You never eat. You never sleep. How did I not see it? It's as plain as the nose on your *face*. I can't believe it took me this long!"

"Because you were not meant to," Jeeves responded calmly.

"What am I missing here?" Pepper asked, looking back and forth between us.

Martin stared, his face white.

I took down my wards, shields, and every other magical wrapping I had cocooned myself in since I arrived at Mystic's End and looked at Jeeves with every sense I possessed. My powers yawned and stretched outside of their confinements, suddenly free to breathe.

That Jeeves was paranormal was clear now.

But there was more.

The magical spells and glamours wrapped around him like so many webs and blankets glimmered and shined. Dense, layered magic designed to hide what he was from the world.

"I can explain," Martin said simply. I looked at him to double check *he* was human. He was.

Truth be told, I was a little shocked.

"Explain what?" Pepper asked, confused.

"Are my friends safe with you?" I asked Jeeves.

"They are," he answered.

"Upstairs," I spat at Martin. "Now."

* * *

G ideon watched intently from the bed as Martin stood across the room from me.

"Talk," I told him.

"Jeeves—Chris—is a vampire," Martin told me.

"No kidding!" I exclaimed angrily. I didn't bring him up here to the third floor so he could confess the things I had figured out on my own. "How about telling me something I *don't* know?"

Martin looked like a man having a severe struggle with himself. After a silence that lasted almost a full minute, he said, "Look, when you couldn't tell what he was initially, I figured the enchantments we put around him—"

"We. Who's *we*?"

"Are you going to let me explain?" Martin asked with exasperation.

"Who's. We," I demanded again.

"My family—"

"You have witches *in your family?*" I asked dumbfounded. "I may not be *much* of a witch, Martin, and I may be new to all of this—but I *know* what witch magic looks like. That vampire's wrapped up like a seven-layer burrito in some of the most complicated magical spells I've *ever* seen. Those are not simple spells."

"They change, or mask, some of his vampiric nature," he admitted. "That's why he can go outside in the sun, why he's not pale. If you listen to his heartbeat, he'll have one. He even feels warm to the touch."

"But he's bulletproof and powerful," I guessed.

Martin nodded. "The perfect guard."

"How on earth did you get a vampire to *agree* to guard you?" I asked him.

Martin shifted on his feet. After a few seconds, he met my eyes. "Chris agreed to become a vampire to take this job," Martin admitted. "His family was given an enormous sum of money in exchange for a certain number of years of service, and we...well, he...Fortuna, *stop* looking at me like that."

"Like *what?*" I asked coldly.

"It was *his* choice."

"You bribed him! You bribed him with an impossible choice to *give up his life!*"

"It's not like that!" Martin yelled back. "See,

this is why I never told you! I *knew* you wouldn't understand."

"He couldn't have been more than *twenty-five* when he was turned," I told him.

"We gave him immortality!"

"You gave him death and servitude," I flung back at him.

"How is this *any* different from what happened to you?" Martin asked defensively. "No. You know what? It *is* different. *He* was able to give his family a life of leisure, free from worry. A gift most people never have the opportunity to give. *You* were forced to make a choice when the paranormal world came after you and said *you* didn't deserve to live. *You* had to turn or die. *He* turned to give his family a life and himself immortality. His being a vampire was far more self-actualizing than *your* witch-by-knife-point conversion!"

Rage coursed through my veins—which, considering I had unwrapped and unfurled my power, was dangerous.

For him.

"How many are there?" I asked quietly.

"How many what?"

"How many paranormals does your family...*employ?*"

Martin pushed himself off the dresser he had been leaning against. His face was serious, his eyes troubled. "I can't tell you that," he said. The guilty flush on his face betrayed the numbers he was trying to hide.

"And all of them willingly just *gave* up their lives?"

"In exchange for—"

"Stop, just stop," I told him, holding my hand up. "I can't listen anymore."

"I've been around those like you *all* my life," Martin said firmly stepping closer. "I didn't want to lie to you. And, to be honest, I don't believe I have. I just didn't tell you the whole truth. I wanted you to get to know me first, to understand—"

"I just spent the last couple of years of my life fighting for the *freedom* of paranormals to choose," I told Martin just as firmly. "I risked my life for that *more* than once. I've known all species and creatures, all different people. The one thing they all wanted was the right to *choose*."

"Chris had the right to choose, Fortuna—"

"You can't tell me, not seriously, that he had any *real* idea what he was committing to. And now?" I asked him, my voice cold. "If he decided tomorrow that he didn't want to be your manservant, that he wanted more of a life than his twenty-four-seven trailing of you? Would he be free to leave?"

Martin looked at me silently.

"Or would you, or your family, claw back the

gift from *his* family? Would you take back some or all of the things you used to bribe him into becoming your soldier?"

His expression told me everything I needed to know.

"Fortuna—"

"If that's the case, Martin, Jeeves doesn't really have a choice at all, does he? None of them, in the end, *really* have a choice. How long are they required to serve your family? Just long enough for the people they *personally* care about to live their human lives and pass on? Are you all that careful? That calculated?"

Martin's eyes were clouded with pain. "Fortuna—"

"Get out," I whispered, tears filling my eyes. "You made your fortune on paranormals you controlled. Your family...Just get out, Martin."

We stood facing one another. Gideon watched us both. The dog was silent in the middle of a moment I couldn't believe I was having. How had I been so stupid? How could I have developed feelings for someone that could do such a thing to others? It wasn't slavery, but not *that* far from it.

"I'm going to go," he said, leaning away from me. "I'm going to give you some time to calm down and process what you've learned. I think if you really think about it, Fortuna, you'll understand it's not as bad as you think it is. And even if it is, *I'm not my family*."

It was late, and I was tired. It'd been a long day, and my head was spinning from the barrage of information I had uncovered without meaning to. Without looking. Without wanting to know.

"Go home, Martin," I said wearily.

"Good night, Fortuna," he replied.

Then he left.

TWELVE

I tossed and turned, thinking, for what felt like hours until I finally drifted off to sleep.

The dog had *no* such issues.

Opening my eyes the following morning, my vision cleared to a cheerful wash of sunlight and a wet dog nose millimeters from my face. Gideon's cheerful, smiling open mouth exhaled humid, bacon-scented air up my nose.

"Ugh, your breath is *not* what I want in my face first thing in the morning," I mumbled, turning away. He snorted happily in response and pressed against my back. "We need to brush your teeth, dude." The happy snorting stopped short as I heard Gideon's jaw snap shut. "Relax. I'm not jumping out of bed to do it now."

My mood, after yesterday, was dark. It felt like the sunny morning light flooding my chipper pink bedroom was mocking me.

A heart appeared in my mind. Then another. Then another.

"I love you, too, dog," I told Gideon softly. Rolling back over, I stuck my arm out around the loving hound and kissed him on the nose.

He sneezed in my face.

"Ugh!" I jerked back. Wiping my face off with the duvet, I sat up and rubbed my eyes to find Spike floating at the end of my bed. "Jeez, can you *knock?*"

"I heard what happened last night, I just wanted to check on you and see if you were okay." He drifted down to sit on the end of the bed cross-legged, his chin in his hand. Gideon inched down excitedly toward the ghost and wagged his tail happily.

"How on earth did *you* find out what happened?"

"Pepper called Liz because she was worried. Then she put her on speakerphone so I could hear what happened."

"What's Pepper worried about?" I asked, frowning.

"You."

"I don't know why anyone would be worried

about me," I said as I pulled back the duvet and got out of bed. "It's not like I didn't have my reservations about Martin, anyway. The fact that he *enslaves vampires* isn't exactly unexpected."

"Weird, I don't *see* one." Spike leaned over the bed, his eyes searching the floor.

"See what?"

"The shark you're jumping."

I glared at him. "Ha ha. *You've* come a long way from the snotty teen with a mohawk that I dug out of a wall."

"Yes, well...." Spike shrugged with a smile. "I guess when you're dead maturity comes pretty fast. Sucks it doesn't work that way when you're alive."

I glared at him again. "Was that a crack at me?"

"No," he said with surprise. "Why would you think that?

"Criminy, you all really *are* worried about me. You're positively pleasant."

"You seem like you're in a pretty bad mood. And, frankly, we haven't spent much time together lately." Spike shrugged again. "I've changed a little, you know. Oh! Speaking of people that you don't know as well as you think you do," he pivoted, "I think claiming Martin enslaves vampires is a *bit* of an overreaction."

"I don't, but I'll bite." Spike winced and slapped

his hand to his face. "Oops. No pun intended. Why's that?"

"Because you haven't talked to *the vampire*," Spike said as he crossed his arms. "You've made this about Martin, Fortuna, but it's *not* about Martin. It's about Jeeves, or Chris, or whatever he wants to be called. You're passing judgment without *ever* getting his side of the story."

"First, Martin talked *for* Jeeves last night, so it sure as heck *is* about Martin. And two, I've seen this kind of thing before—"

"No, you *haven't*," Spike disagreed, cutting me off. "This *isn't* your circus. This is Mystic's End, Arkansas. You're getting what happened with Jeeves all wrapped up in your past experiences. You fought with *gods*, Fortuna. I can *guarantee* you no gods are running around this dump of a town. This isn't the paranormal world—this is *one small town*. It's *not* the same thing. You're trying to make it the same thing, but it's *not*."

"Okay, enough. I haven't even had my coffee yet, Spike," I told him wearily as I eyed my bed and contemplated crawling back into it.

"Just think about it, will you?" Gideon thrust an image of a giant brain pulsing in my head, and I wondered where on earth the dog saw a brain so he was able to recreate such an image.

"Quit ganging up on me," I told Gideon. "Let

me get a shower and some coffee. Go."

Spike and Gideon left the bedroom, but Spike's words hung in the air.

* * *

Walking in with my coffee, I turned to look at the clock on the storefront wall at the same time Azalea said, "I opened on time, no worries." She looked surprised to see me. The feeling was mutual—I hadn't realized until then just how late I'd slept.

Thank goodness for Azalea.

"Thanks so much. Yesterday was a *weird* day," I said, throwing the keys back under the counter. "Any sign of Zach Johnson?"

"No," she said quietly, her face showing the shadow of a pout. "And I even saw Mrs. Johnson come in this morning to get her hair done at Liz's. I wonder what he's doing? I mean, there's not much to do in this town, really."

"Is he over twenty-one? Because if he is, that's not *quite* the case," I pointed out.

Azalea shook her head no. "He's nineteen."

The bells on my front door jingled, and I turned, hoping for Azalea's sake it was Zach.

It was not. It was Jeeves. I didn't see Martin behind him.

"Good morning," I said, nodding to the vampire.

"Can we talk?" he asked me quietly from the other side of the room.

I had shrouded myself in protections again, and Jeeves looked the same as he always had. Tall, handsome, with eyes piercing in their intensity. My gaze settled on his mouth for a moment. No fangs. And yet I knew it was unlikely that mouth had not bitten someone and drained them of their life. I mean, why else be a vampire?

"If we talk, I'll be happy to tell you," he answered.

I frowned.

"Fortuna?" Azalea quietly asked, sensing the tension in the room.

"Talk to him," Spike said as he floated into the room. I saw Jeeves' eyes flicker over toward him, and then back to my face.

He was a telepath. And he could see ghosts. Could he hear them, too?

"Yes," Jeeves responded calmly.

Oh boy.

"Fortuna—" Spike started, but I cut him off with a wave.

"Come on," I said, waving him to follow. "You got the front, Azalea? You need anything?"

"I'm good. Take as long as you need," she said

quietly, her eyes on Jeeves as he stalked silently through the store to follow. He nodded kindly to her, then smiled. Her tense muscles seemed to relax as if he sprinkled *I'm okay, you're okay* dust on her.

What powers did this man *have*?

I guess I was about to find out.

* * *

"Was that a vampire trick?" I asked him quietly once we were on the second floor.

"There are times when humans perceive danger when they look at me, even if they don't know *quite* what that danger is." Jeeves nodded as I invited him to sit. "It's a simple thing to make them feel lulled into comfort or force them to be at ease again. If I choose to."

"We had no vampires at the circus, so I never met one."

"My kind were not welcome at the circuses, or so I've been told," Jeeves said. "We are solitary creatures and creatures that kill for survival. I can understand why others would prefer that we stay far from their towns and encampments."

"Do you?" I asked curiously.

"Kill?"

I nodded.

"I do. I don't nourish myself *exclusively* through

killing. But yes," he admitted without concern,
"I do."

I examined him again, not sure what to ask him.
The paranormal world I came from had strict rules
—no killing of other paranormals. No killing of
humans. These things were punishable by death
when the Witches' Council was in charge and were
punishable by imprisonment now that the
paranormal world adopted a more democratic
system. How had Jeeves and his kind *escaped* those
rules? I had so many questions I didn't even know
where to start.

"Then let me start, and tell you what I sense
you wish to know," Jeeves said as he sat back. "Yes, I
can see Spike." He turned and smiled at the silent
ghost. Spike nodded back, his eyes wide. "I can see
him because I am, in essence, just another form of
what he is. I am a spirit tied to the physical world by
this body."

"How are you—"

"I can read your mind because this body is tied
to the web of life through the blood I consume. The
more I consume, the stronger the power, the more
unbreakable the tie."

"I don't understand."

"We are all related by blood. Some closer, some
farther apart. The more diverse the blood I
consume, the more connected I am to those webs.

The more I can see within them. Blood contains an amazing amount of information," he explained. "Did you know mothers live their lives with cells of their offspring circulating through their veins? Scientists don't know why they stay a part of her. But it is a simple, yet profound, example of how we are connected by blood."

"So, you just traveled around the world, killing as many seemingly unrelated people as possible to expand your power?" I asked horrified.

"Vampires are more sophisticated than you might think," Jeeves said, his eyes twinkling. "And your own people have assisted us over the years."

"*My* people?"

"Witches."

Oh, right. My people.

"Just like you can duplicate a brick in a wall, so, too, could you duplicate the cells of blood to make more. No one has to die to feed us."

I stared at him. "Then why kill?"

"Some people need killing," Jeeves said with a tilt of the head.

"You're kind of scary," Spike observed. From way across the other side of the room.

"I mean you no harm," Jeeves said with a smile friendlier than I thought him capable of. "And even if I did, you're a ghost. You have no weaknesses I could exploit."

"But *I* do," I pointed out. "And so do my friends."

"That's true from a *certain* perspective." He nodded. "You have a natural fear of me. It *is* understandable. The tie-in to the web of witches is certainly a tempting one to sip from. However, we have our own set of rules, and so from another perspective, you have nothing to fear from me."

"Why's that?"

"We *need* you," he said simply. "Your witch magic is *our* fountain of youth. Without witches, we would *have* to kill to survive. Many of us have no taste for robbing others of their life. Especially those of us that were turned against their will. It's a symbiotic relationship that has worked for thousands of years."

And yet, I never met one. I was warned to stay away from vampires.

"I didn't say *all* witches entered into this symbiotic relationship," Jeeves pointed out as he addressed the fleeting thought in my mind. "You are right, the vast majority despise and fear us. And so most of us live in the human world."

"You say us like vampires are your people—"

"They are."

"But you got turned to take the job with Martin," I said, shifting the discussion from a general vampire education to the specifics of Jeeves' experience. "It sounded to me like you got bribed to turn, too. And that you can't quit. *And* you had to know I was a witch from the moment you saw me since you're a telepath—how could you not say anything! How could *he* not tell me?"

"As I just told you, while we do work *with* witches, not *all* witches feel that my kind are paranormals worth the cost of our existence," Jeeves said, a flash of pain darkening his expression. "Martin did not know which type of witch you were. He withheld that information to protect me."

"Protect you from what?"

"From you."

"From *me*?" I asked, shocked. That Martin thought I could be some kind of murdering witch out to tear the heads off vampires was offensive.

"Fortuna, *you* were the one that said the guy was wrapped in magic, so much so that you couldn't even tell what he was," Spike said, moving closer to the vampire. "There *must* be witches that would harm vampires or something. And I would guess they *can*. Otherwise, why go to the trouble of hiding what they are *from* witches?"

"Your ghost friend is correct," Jeeves nodded. "We are, obviously, not immune to your magic. It can help us hide in plain sight, but it can also destroy us if the caster chooses to try."

"You know," I said, sitting down with a thump.

"I came here to get *away* from all this garbage."

"I do know," Jeeves admitted. "I can see it in your m—"

"Oh, shut up," I told him absently.

I sat silently and tried to process yet another Mystic's End revelation.

"Fortuna," Jeeves said quietly as he reached out a hand across the counter and lightly covered mine with it. "No one forced me to become what I am. Martin doesn't force me to serve as his confidant, his friend, *or* his guard. He is like a brother to me, and we are connected by—"

"Oh my gosh, you *drank his blood*," I whispered, paling as my stomach churned. "You did, didn't you?"

"I did." He smiled. "And due to that, we are connected. I will always know when he is in danger, or when he is in pain...like now."

"A vampire is one hell of a wingman to have," Spike observed quietly. "No pun intended."

"Someday, as we get to know one another, as we become friends," Jeeves said, squeezing my hand, "perhaps I will tell you why I made the choice I did. Why I decided to become what I am. *If* you wish to know." I nodded. "But that's not a story I am comfortable sharing with you today. What I need you to know from today are two things."

"And those are?"

"One? No one forced me to be who I am, any more than anyone forced you to become who you are." He looked at me knowingly. "Despite what Martin said last night out of pain, you and I both know that we *could* have made other choices. We didn't. Don't disrespect my choice by claiming it was coerced."

Well, that was straightforward enough. "I'm sorry," I said, and he waved it away.

"I understand *why* you said what you said, more than you think. But I am telling you that I did what I did because it was what I wanted. No one made me do what I did. Do you agree to accept that as truth?"

I hesitated, but only for a moment. "Agreed."

"And two, Martin is a good man at heart. Yes, he came from a family that tried to bend him into someone without morals, without conscience," Jeeves said, withdrawing his hand. "But he stands against that as hard as he can. I'm not asking you to love him back—"

Love him *back?*

"—but I am asking you to cut him *slightly* more slack than you have. He cares for you deeply. And that means *I* care for you deeply because of our bond. Just don't be so hard on him?"

I nodded as if in a daze.

Love him *back?*

THIRTEEN

"Well, that's convenient," Pepper said as she picked up all the notes from the table and tossed them in the trash. "I guess we won't need any of this work from yesterday since it's all pretty useless now." She chuckled. "At least I got to spend time with Ollie doing all that useless stuff."

I balled my fists up and fought the urge to punch her in the nose. "What the heck are you *doing?*"

"We were narrowing down suspects," Pepper pointed to the trashcan. "Why even bother? We have a vampire that was around *every single one* of those people. Did you ask him about what he thinks happened to the urn?"

"Did I...what the...I swear you shift gears faster than anyone I've ever met before!" I told her. Leaning over, I unclenched my fists and dug the papers out of the trash. My hand plunged into wet coffee grounds, and I cringed.

Pepper stood with her hand on her hip, watching me dumpster-dive into my own garbage can. Her eyes were sparkling with excitement now that we were no longer talking about my feelings about Martin. A conversation that lasted maybe all of five minutes. A conversation that careened to a screeching halt when I mentioned Jeeves' incredible telepathic ability. "Look, we have a *vampire* now."

"He's not a pet!" I told her hotly.

"No, but Martin is working on this whole missing urn thing with us. Isn't he? Spike told Liz through that ghost app you talked to Jeeves, everything is copacetic, *and* we still have a missing urn to find, right? We are going to still work on that, right? Oh, of course, we are," Pepper answered for me, jabbering so I couldn't get a word in edgewise. Just as I was about to respond, she continued. "Only now, Fortuna, we have a vampire to help! And not just *any* vampire! A super-duper telepathic vampire that's been around *all* the people you're digging out of the trash, and who doesn't have your stuck-up-edness about digging around in people's—"

"Stuck-*up-edness*?" I snapped as I shook the grounds off the papers.

"I just made it up," Pepper said proudly, and then looked at Gideon. "Can you believe I know a witch *and* a vampire, dog? Ooh!" Her eyes widened, and she spun toward me. "Do you know any fairies? I *always* wanted to meet a fairy. Are they really super-small, like Tinkerbell? Because the thing about vampires not coming out during the day doesn't seem to be true." She frowned. "Do you think he sleeps in a coffin? Wait—do you think he sleeps *at all*?"

That urge to crawl back into bed was getting stronger.

"What time's Martin coming over?" Pepper asked.

"I don't know if he is."

"What do you mean, you don't know if he is?"

"I'm still...processing, I guess." I shrugged as I finished cleaning the last of the papers and stacked them back on the table. "I don't know if I'm ready to see Martin yet."

Pepper whistled and looked me up and down. "Damn, girl, you're *brave*, breaking your word to a vampire. Didn't you promise him you'd cut his buddy Martin some slack?"

"Stop cursing."

"That's not even a curse, prude."

"The last twenty-four hours changed everything I understood about this town," I told her, my exasperation creeping toward anger. "Crazy cult people at the church acting like they played extras in *Children of the Corn*. Who, incidentally, know about paranormals somehow. Now a psychic vampire. And that's on *top* of the stupid book that crawled up out of the earth on its own. To show me one single page telling me to scry, as well. I swear, I think the circus was quieter."

"You're starting to sound like me that night," Pepper said with a mouth full of muffin. "Funny how our attitudes have switched, huh? Now *you're* the one all freakin' out and stuff, and I'm like *invite the vampire over*! That's funny, huh, Fortuna?"

"Hysterical," I deadpanned.

Gideon barked.

* * *

I slid behind the wheel and turned the van on. I was heading over to Mystic Memories.

Alone.

It was probably way, way past time I sat down and had a heart to heart with Miss Bessie, and I didn't want to do it with anyone else around. Not Gideon. Not Pepper. Not Spike. Just me.

Just me and her, alone.

Suddenly, I jumped as a thought invaded my mind—did Jeeves know about her, too?

Well, I mean, obviously he knew *of* her, I thought as I turned on the road that would take me toward the home. How close did he need to be to us to read minds? Did he know that she was the Mystic's End mystic and that now *I* was? Did he know more about me than *I* did because of his powers? Just what kind of psychic abilities did vampires have, anyway?

I brought my hand to my neck and felt the smooth, soft skin. The artery pulsed beneath my fingertips, and I shivered. "Calm down, Fortuna," I told myself. I pulled into the parking lot, found a spot, and put the van in park. "Other paranormals have a right to live anywhere they want now. It's not like you *didn't* know you could run into one now and again."

A knock on my window interrupted my self-lecture. I looked up to see Rick Taylor, the handsome nurse from Mystic Memories (who also happened to be kind of a jerk).

Great, just what I needed.

I turned the car off and pushed the door open.

He jumped back. "Hey, are you okay?" Rick asked, smiling.

I gave him a strange look. Rick and were not exactly on friendly terms after he railed on me for giving a girl he was crushing on information about her recently deceased husband.

"Fine." Rick bobbed his head and waited for me to continue, but I didn't.

"So, I thought I saw you talking to yourself. Unless you were talking to a ghost or something," he joked cheerfully. "With you, I guess no one ever really knows."

Har, har.

"Was just talking through some stuff," I told him. I locked up the van and turned to face him. "Something I can do for you?"

"Me? No, no, just getting off my shift and saw you pull in. Thought I'd say hi. See how you were and all." Rick smiled again, and I realized that he was trying to charm me. "So, how *are* you doing?"

"I'm fine, Rick." I tilted my head. "I didn't think you and I were on friendly terms anymore, after the situation with Emily."

"Oh, that," he wheezed, rolled his eyes and shrugged like he hadn't yelled at me for messing up his chances with a widow. I fought the urge to roll *my* eyes. "It was just a tense time with Emily and

Lulu and the stuff with Tom. I wasn't *really* angry with you or anything. Right?"

"Are you *asking* me if you were really angry with me?"

"Yeah, no, I mean, I'm *telling* you. I was just tense and all, you know?"

Tense was one way to put it, I guess.

"So, listen," he said, but I cut him off.

"Look, Rick, I have to go see Miss Bessie and then head back to the store. Can we talk another time?" I asked, and then gestured toward the home. "I don't have a lot of time."

A flicker of irritation flashed across his face, and then he swallowed his frustration. "Sure, sure, absolutely." Rick nodded. "Let's talk the next time you come and teach a class, maybe?"

"Maybe," I nodded noncommittally. "See you, Rick!"

As he called out a good-bye, I made a mental note to ask Miss Bessie whether Rick and Emily had ever got together. I was sure Rick was borderline hitting on me again—and I wasn't sure being in a relationship with Emily would have stopped him.

* * *

"A vampire?" Miss Bessie asked, her head bobbing. "Well, *that* makes a lot of sense now, doesn't it? It explains a lot. Oh, indeed, it does." The old woman's eyes lit up as if she had just solved a puzzle that had long frustrated her.

"Does it?" I sat in her private room, the door closed, at a small two-person table. "I'm not sure I follow."

"I knew there *had* to be a reason Martin Salvi seemed to know everything before anyone else in the town. He may well be the only one with more gossip than *I* have, and *he* doesn't share his," Miss Bessie said with a knowing nod, brushing her palms together. "The track always seemed to be one step ahead of everyone else on business, with the politicians. Martin having a vampire in tow? That'd do it."

".Should I be worried?"

"Worried about what, dear, the vampire?" I nodded. The old woman waved away my concern. "Heavens, no. You could blast that nightwalker with a pinky finger covered in molasses while you're drunk, you could." Then she tilted her head. "That's not to say he doesn't have a lot of arrows in his quiver. Vampires are powerful, powerful telepaths. Much more powerful than you are."

"All of them?"

"Depends on how much, how often, and how

varied they drink, dear. From what you told me, it sounds like Jeeves is a soldier vampire. I imagine he's taken steps to make sure he has as *many* powers as he can, and that they're topped up regularly." Miss Bessie frowned. "Didn't your circus friends ever tell you about vampires?"

"Just that I should stay away from them." I lifted my shoulder in a half shrug. "I picked up what I could when I could, but I never got training. Honestly, I think Ollie may have got more training than I did. And he's human."

"I didn't get any training, either, dear," the old woman said as she reached across and patted my hand with her bony one. "You make do with what you have, and you're young. You'll learn. So, tell Miss Bessie the truth now. Did you come all the way out here just to tell me about the vampire?"

"Well, that was part of it," I told her, my eyes on my lap. I exhaled nervously. "I went to the Holy Grove Church the other night and talked to—"

"Beulah, Tula and Tallulah?" she asked knowingly. I glanced up. "Word travels fast around here, girl. Some of the old biddies here are members of that wretched church, you know."

"So I'm not wrong. There's something odd about that place, right?"

"Oh, odd ain't the half of it, Fortuna." She turned her face away and gazed out the window toward the church as if she could see it through the trees. After a few moments, she turned back and stared at me. My breaths quickened. "Are you sure you're ready?"

"I don't know how to answer that, honestly," I admitted. Miss Bessie waited, watching me. My chest rose and fell, rose and fell as I thought about my answer, and she waited for me to commit. Finally, I looked down at my hands and stared at the flesh as it rose and divided around the bones. Jeeves was more bound to humanity than I was. He was connected by blood he drank. I was connected to...nothing. Only that which I chose. Was I ready? I hugged myself, suddenly cold, and then looked up.

Miss Bessie asked again. "Are you sure you're ready?"

I nodded.

"You need to say it, Fortuna," she told me gently.

"I'm ready," I said aloud, my voice catching. "Tell me."

FOURTEEN

"Do you know how this town was founded?" Miss Bessie asked. "Did I tell you about it?"

I shook my head no. Miss Bessie shifted in her chair and stared at me, waiting for additional information. "So, Spike told me a *little* bit about it, but not much. I know it was once called Mystic. That some women showed up here to found the town, and the rumor was that they were a coven of witches. But that's pretty much it."

"Rumor? It was no *rumor*," Miss Bessie snorted with contempt. "The women were here before the Abernathy family, before the Kanes. They came here seeking *peace*, a place to live where they wouldn't be bothered." The old woman frowned. "*That* didn't last very long."

"Someone *did* tell me the Abernathy family founded the town. I can't recall who."

"They founded Mystic's *End*, sure. But Mystic's End was *not* the original town."

"Right. The name change. Hey, was it paranormal? The original Mystic, I mean."

"Not in the way I think *you* mean it," Miss Bessie said, pointing out her window. Her eyes grew distant. "This town is as regular as any other in many ways. The girls didn't shift it to a different reality, they didn't make it so humans couldn't come in. They—the women—*were* human. Half-human, in any case. The daughters of witches and mortal men, half-breeds that didn't feel safe in the paranormal world, *or* the human one."

"What happened to them?"

"They were hunted, of course," she answered, her voice thick with sadness. "Like all witches were back in the day. Settlers found a village with a well, buildings, farms. The springs provided fresh water and drew animals they could hunt. The land was fertile. The only thing standing between a pioneer life of ease and the riches of this area was a bunch of hippie women."

"But they were witches," I argued. "Couldn't they defend what they had?"

"Obviously not, dear." Miss Bessie waved her hand again toward the window. "This is no hippie, new age commune you live in."

"You think that's what it would be like if they'd kept control?"

"I don't know. I'd like to think so." She smiled. "But who's to say? The women are long dead, and no one has been able to talk to them for hundreds of years."

My head snapped up. "What do you mean, *talk* to them?"

"Twenty-seven women founded this town," she said, ignoring my question. "Some were killed. Some were taken to wife by the invaders. Some had children already. But every one—every one—had a witch bottle." Miss Bessie looked at me expectantly and sighed at the confused look on my face. "A *witch bottle*, dear. Don't you know what that is?" I shook my head no. "It is a spell contained in a bottle. It is believed that once you bury it, the bottle can capture evil. Or," Miss Bessie shifted uncomfortably, "whatever—or whoever—the bottle is targeting."

"Well, clearly, they don't work," I told her, crossing my arms. "If those bottles were meant to keep out a bunch of invading marauders, they *failed*."

"They *didn't* fail," the old woman snapped as

she shifted again and grunted. "Someone turned the bottles *against* the women, used them to curse *every* one. Twenty-seven bottles against twenty-seven women. Buried to bind them within the confines of their own magic, trapping them in the nature they so loved. If they—or their descendants—so much as *questioned* the descendants of the men," Miss Bessie explained, her eyes narrowing, "they died and were trapped here forever. Their power dispersed into the earth."

"You said trapped in nature," I said, frowning. "Are they just trapped spirits? Or... Okay, what do you mean by *disbursed into the earth*?"

"It's what it sounds like. Their power went into the land here. The land, the trees. Maybe the rocks. They're invisible nature spirits now. Surely you've heard the whispers in the trees? Maybe tripped over a rock you were *sure* wasn't there a minute before?"

I thought of the grove opening the land itself to expel a magic book.

"How many were trapped?" I whispered.

"At least twenty-seven," Miss Bessie shrugged. "Could there be more than one woman in a bottle? Maybe. No one has ever found the bottles to be able to break the spells. As I said, no one has ever been powerful enough to talk to the women to find out how many there are." She looked at me intensely. "Though I suspect that *may* have changed."

"Me?" I asked, shocked. "Why *me*?"

"The descendants of the Delphi Coven have long dissipated whatever power the women had themselves. Naturally, I mean. Since they were half-witches to *begin* with, they weren't playing with a topped up tank, if you get my drift."

"The...*Delphi* Coven..." My heart thumped in my chest as my stomach grew cold.

"Only one in each generation could hold the protection spell, hold the magic still left. A mystic. One who would be told the old stories, one who was charged to remember what everyone else—well, *almost* everyone else—forgot." The old woman's watery eyes blinked. "That was me. Now, it's you."

"We're descendants of this coven? You and me?"

"Different branches, but yes. The only two left with any awareness of it as far as I know. The chain of the curse is broken for future generations if a descendant bears no daughters or is killed by a descendant of the invaders. But those whose souls were trapped already? They are still trapped."

The cold feeling in the pit of my stomach grew. "And Gabe's mother, Mary...she was, too."

"She was." Miss Bessie nodded. "I stayed long, long after my time because Mary was the last of them...us. I suspected I would die a failure, never having found a bottle and never having allowed those women, however many there are, to have their rest."

I wanted to ask if Mary Wilcox was trapped, but I couldn't bring myself to do it. Besides, from what Miss Bessie said, the assumption was yes—but there was no way to be sure.

"What about Gabe? Why not pass the power to him?" I asked her.

"Gabe's a *man*, Fortuna," she said, clucking her tongue. "This is *woman's* magic. Passed mother to daughter, preferably. Passed to the daughter of another descendant if necessary."

"But I *know* male witches. Charlotte's husband is one—"

"You're not *hearing* me," Miss Bessie said as she slapped the table. "This is *not* your normal paranormal world shenanigans here. This is a *curse* laid upon those women and upon the town. I am a witch *only* because my mother made me the mystic, and that act woke powers in me." She leaned forward and pointed her bony finger at me. "You and I, Fortuna—we're *not* the same. Oh, I know, I know, I *said* we were." She rolled her eyes. "But we're not, not really. And the longer it gets from having passed you the power, the less *I* have. I am no longer connected to the town, to nature, the way I was. Within months, I'll have *no* magic at all. I will age and wither like everyone must. Eventually, I'll die."

I registered for the first time that Miss Bessie was moving like an old woman, shifting in her chair with a wince of pain. Just a few months ago, she'd run up a set of stairs two at a time like a spirited teenager (even though she would only do such an unexplainable thing in front of me).

Now, the years seemed to weigh on her.

"Then *why* did you give me the power?" I asked, crestfallen and worried for her. "I was already a witch, I didn't *need* this!"

"Because that's the way of life, child," she told me gently. "And because you are a *full* paranormal witch, something we have *never* had in this town. A descendant of the Delphi Coven with full witch powers? Fortuna, dear, how could I *not* give you the power? You, my dear, were *meant* to return here. You were meant to bring peace to the Delphi Coven. To break the curse. I'm *sure* of it."

As I listened to her, I believed it.

Even though I wasn't sure I did.

Not really.

It all seemed too pat, too destined, too wrapped up in a bow. I *wasn't* Charlotte. I was never chosen for anything in my life, and I had a hard time believing I was some kind of destined witch savior.

For goodness' sake, I wasn't even an *actual* witch until last year!

But Miss Bessie believed. Completely.

And so I tried to believe, too.

"So, what am I supposed to do?" I asked.

"Find the bottles, break them, and save the souls of your ancestors, dear. And your *own* child, should you ever have a daughter," Miss Bessie said as if the answer was obvious. "They obviously trust you to do it. They *gave* you the book."

I nodded, thinking. "Hey, why can't I open the book on my own if I'm some super-descendant destined to save all the ghost women?"

"Because they don't trust you *that* much," Miss Bessie told me with a wink.

* * *

She hadn't told me anything about my birth mother, and I suspected that was by design. I barely had any time to process what she said before there was a knock at the door.

"Come in!" she hollered. "Not like there's any privacy in this damn place, anyway!"

"Gram?" Gabe poked his head in and smiled. "Fortuna." He nodded. "Didn't expect to find you here." Then he frowned. "What's wrong?"

"Why would anything be wrong?" I asked, my voice thick with emotion.

"Because your face is all puffy like you were crying," Gabe said, pointing.

Had I been crying? I touched my cheeks and found they were wet. "Allergies," I told him, wiping my face. "Not used to Arkansas yet, I guess."

"Riiight," he answered, unconvinced.

Dozens of questions were running through my mind. I knew more than I did, but *what* was this power I supposedly had? Miss Bessie didn't explain that. And these bottles. How do I find twenty-seven bottles hidden in the town? And there's a curse—wait, then *who* cast the curse? Did one witch betray the others? Did the clergy dude have magic? And how does Holy Grove Church know about the grove? Or do they? *Is* that the grove? Or are they talking about the woods where the bottles are buried? Ugh, am I going to have to join that *crazy* church to—

"Fortuna?" Gabe snapped his fingers in front of me, and my eyes refocused.

"Sorry, what?" I looked up and was struck for a split-second out of nowhere by Gabe's overpowering masculinity. He was so close I could breathe him in—an outdoorsy scent that reminded me of the forest after it rained. "I'm sorry," I replied, coughing to cover my momentary attraction. "Did you say something?"

"Yeah, I asked if you wanted to go out to lunch with Gram and me," he said, giving me an odd look. "Are you *sure* you're okay? You look a little pale."

"Gabe, darling, could you get me a glass of ice water? And *not* the ice water from the hallway," Miss Bessie asked him while waving him toward the door. "The good cups from the cafeteria. The ice is colder in there, anyway."

"Colder ice, right," Gabe answered dubiously. "Fortuna, can I get you anything?"

I shook my head no.

"Okay, be back in about five minutes," he said. Looking at his grandmother, Gabe added, "Is that enough time for you to go over what you need to without my being in here? Or should I run to the convenience store down the hill to get your ice water?"

"Don't you sass me, boy," Miss Bessie said gruffly.

"Yes, ma'am." Gabe smiled at her affectionately, bowing his head. Then he left the room, gently closing the door behind him.

"I know you have questions, and I have more to tell you," Miss Bessie said quickly after the door clicked. "But for now, this is what you *need* to know. The other side has descendants, too," she said, her eyes burning with anger. "I know you've barely noticed the change in you since I made you mystic. That's a consequence of you *already* being a full-fledged witch. You *do* have mystic powers, though—they just don't seem special to you because, for the most part, you already *had* many of those same abilities."

"But—"

"And those powers can be *passed*."

"Right, you told me that—"

"And anything that can be *given*, Fortuna, can also be *taken*," Miss Bessie said, bobbing her head. "You understand? Anything one person can give to another, someone else can *take* if they have a mind to. One person's *magic* is another person's *miracle*."

"The Holy Grove Church," I guessed.

Miss Bessie nodded vigorously. "You've already shined a light on yourself by waltzing in here with the name *Delphi*," Miss Bessie warned me. Her eyes flashed toward the door, and then back. "I have no doubt they're *already* looking at you. *Wondering* if I passed the power. You can keep them guessing a little because I still have some power, and you were a well-known psychic before you *ever* got here—"

"Well, I wouldn't say *well* known." I blushed with embarrassment.

"—so all your whoozy-whatsis isn't that suspicious. That, and—"

"No one knows I was the foundling on the steps," I finished.

"Exactly." Miss Bessie tilted her head. "If we're lucky, we'll be able to find all the bottles and break the curse before they ever know what's what."

"Are they"—whoever *they* were—"looking for them, too?"

"No doubt." She nodded. "They don't want those women set free."

"Why not? And who's *they*—"

"If you were cooped up in dirt for two hundred years, what would *you* want to do to the descendant of the jerk that put you there?" Miss Bessie threw her hands in the air. "They don't *have* to move on. They can stay here and haunt those that wronged them until they drive 'em batty or put 'em six feet under. We can rename the town *Poltergeist's Revenge*." She paused. "Well, that's if they can even get out of here *to* move on."

"Spike says there are no other ghosts in the town, so some ghosts *have* to be able to get out, I would think," I told her.

"None? None at all?"

"Well, I've seen him and Tom Wilson, but that's it." I shrugged. "No one else."

The doorknob turned.

"Gabe's back. You remember what I said," Miss

Bessie hissed. "Don't you dig up more snakes than you can kill. Don't tell anyone about—"

"But I—"

"No one!"

* * *

It *was* the one secret I'd kept vigilantly.

Since I moved from the circus to Mystic's End, I'd admitted I was psychic. Eventually, I outed myself to my close friends as a witch. Most knew I was adopted.

None knew I was abandoned as an infant in this town.

Not Pepper. Not Gabe. Not Martin. Not Ollie. No one.

Pepper, for all her paranormal blogging and tin hat conspiracy theories, knew nothing about the mystic of Mystic's End. She never asked me why I was chosen, and had been just as curious about what Miss Bessie would say about it as I was.

Gabe knew nothing about the mystic at all. Even though it was his grandmother for *all* of his life.

Well, until I showed up.

Ollie knew what he'd been taught by Priestess Goodfellow in Austin, and what he'd learned at the Holy Grove Church. He'd never given me any indication he knew anything Miss Bessie had just shared with me. Or who I was beyond who I'd been when I moved here.

Well, except the whole *abandoned as a baby in this town* thing.

Martin...

Well, knowing Jeeves was a walking Mystic's End surveillance unit, I couldn't really be clear *what* Martin knew and what he didn't. It's a good thing I wrapped myself in bindings that even *I* had trouble taking off to use my own powers. Maybe he didn't know.

It might be the only reason *they* hadn't come after me.

Yet.

Mystic's End.

Don't you dig up more snakes than you can kill.

Suddenly, the town name seemed as ominous as Charlotte once warned me it was.

FIFTEEN

When I heard another knock on my van window, I thought about ignoring it. I had no interest in another conversation with Rick.

"Fortuna?" I turned and saw Gabe leaning his weight against the door and grinning.

"Yeah, Gabe, what's up?" I asked him after cracking the window. "Need something?"

"I feel like we haven't seen each other in a week."

"Honestly, I don't think we have, not really." I rolled the window the rest of the way down. "The last time I saw you was when you stopped by the shop. You know, when you and Martin basically peed on my leg to mark your territory."

Gabe laughed a big, booming laugh. "You caught that, did you?"

"It wasn't subtle. Did you like poking hornets' nests as a kid?"

"Oh, Martin's not a hornet." Gabe waved his hand as if dismissing the idea a rich mafia prince with a vampire guard could be anything *but* a pussycat. "He's more like...more like a bee. Sure, he *can* sting, but he's really trying to pollinate. Which is good."

Right. A bee *guarded* by a murder hornet.

His answer was...weird, though. I swear Martin and Gabe had such a bizarre on-again, off-again love-hate relationship you'd think *they* were dating.

"I thought you were going to go to lunch with Miss Bessie?"

"My grandmother decided she didn't want to go eat after all." Gabe rolled his eyes as he leaned casually against my van. "She did, however, *encourage* me to race out here and check on you. Said you got some news that might have rattled you a little bit, and that you might need a friend." His eyes held mine, concern shining. "You *did* race out of there pretty fast."

"I'm fine." I wasn't, not really. But how could I explain to Gabe what I learned? I couldn't. Not without outing that Miss Bessie had been hiding who she was from him his entire life. It wasn't my place to tell him, but until he knew, I could share none of this with him.

Secrets.

Secrets never amounted to anything good.

"Forgive me for saying so, but you don't look like you're fine. Come on," Gabe said, jerking his head toward town. "Let me take you out to lunch. Whatever's going on, it can't be that bad."

As I followed Gabe to the diner in my van, I wondered if he would feel the same way if he knew that his mother's soul might be trapped in a tree.

* * *

The Mystic Diner was packed when we arrived. Gabe nodded and shook hands with other police as we walked past their booths. Once we sat down, the waitress beelined to us and took our order with a military level of efficiency. We had barely answered *no* to the question *Anything else?* before she practically ripped the menus from our hands and turned on her heel toward the kitchen.

"So," Gabe said once she left.

"So."

"What news did you get that rattled you?" he asked.

I shook my head. "I can't really talk about it with you. Honestly, I wish I could." And I meant it.

There was something comfortable—most of the time—about talking things through with Gabe. "But, I can't."

"Finally a Mystic's End resident, I see." Gabe smiled warmly.

"What do you mean?"

"Keeping *secrets*," he whispered and then chuckled. "There are secrets large and small all over this town—heck, Arcadia County—just like crystal veins are running through the mountains. In case you haven't figured it out, it's the town pastime. Gossip and secrets."

"In addition to gambling, strippers, and crystal digging?" I joked. "Where *does* everyone find the time? Speaking of secrets, detective—spill."

Gabe raised an eyebrow.

"You and Pepper, obviously."

Gabe laughed. "Not *that* obvious. I figured she would have given you the scoop on that by now. I told you what happened." He shrugged. "There's really not that much more to tell. We care about each other, enjoy spending time together, but that romantic spark? It's just not there anymore."

"It *seemed* like it was there when you flung yourself on top of her a few months ago in my shop."

"Is that a little *jealousy* I hear in your voice?" Gabe asked suggestively. It was a good thing he winked because I was tempted to reach across and punch him in his chiseled patrician nose.

"It's *not* jealousy. Frankly, I'm not interested in dating *anyone* right now." Or, like, maybe never. Discovering the *men* in this town have no problem cursing and *eternally imprisoning* the *women* in this town in rocks and trees is enough to encourage anyone to stay single. "I have a man in my life. Sure, he drools, and his breath smells like bacon most of the time, but for now, that's enough of a relationship for me."

Gabe frowned. "I thought you went on a date with Martin again? Pepper mentioned it was pretty recent."

"I did. Well, sort of."

"Sort of?"

"I mean, I *guess* it was a date." Now that I thought back on it, it was more like getting hired for a job, really. "Something happened when I was at Martin's—actually, a few things—that are making me reclassify the evening retroactively. So, if it was *intended* as a date, it didn't really turn out like one."

Gabe stared at me. "You've lost me."

"Something's missing from Martin's house." I shrugged. "He asked me to help find it, that's all."

Gabe nodded. "The thing Ollie's helping you with. The urn, was it?"

"How'd you know?"

"He *is* my best friend. How much does Pepper hide from you?"

"Not much."

Gabe smiled. "Well, there you go."

"Fortuna!" a gruff voice wheezed. I looked up to find Uncle Vito, Martin Salvi's uncle, staring down at me. Several steps behind him was Harold Whatnow.

"Uncle Vito! Harold." I nodded and smiled. Gabe greeted the two old men with gentle handshakes. "What are you two doing here?"

"I lost a bet," Harold grumbled, his wrinkled face looking glum.

"A bet?" I asked, confused.

"I told this curmudgeonly old coot that Josie Roberts was teasing him all the time because she had a crush on him, though the Lord above only knows *why*," Uncle Vito said, nodding. "If I was right, he had to agree to let me tutor him in charmin' women. If I was wrong—well, who cares what I woulda lost. I didn't and never would. I only make sure bets." Uncle Vito lifted his cap off his head, placed it back down, and winked at me.

"Well, that was very nice of you, Mr. Salvatore," Gabe said to the older man.

"Nice?" Vito snorted. "Nothin' nice about it. Some competition at the home might spice up the days, is all. And maybe if Whatnow gets some tail, he'll stop being such a miserable old codger to be around, though I doubt it." Uncle Vito wheezed, the wheeze turning into a cough. "Pardon me," he apologized. "The COPD is a PITA."

"Stop talkin' all fancy with your letters. You don't know a widget from a whangdoodle. Maybe I'll get lucky, and you'll drop *dead* before you make it to the booth," Harold Whatnow muttered miserably.

"You'd like that, wouldn't you, you miserable old geezer," Uncle Vito shot back. "Bafangu chooch," he muttered to himself. Gabe covered his mouth to hide a laugh.

"*What* did you say?" Harold bellowed at the smaller man.

"It was a blessing on your house, you moron."

"I don't *have* a house—"

"Let's go and let the kids eat their lunch." The waitress whipped around the two men and unloaded plates from a tray onto the table. "You two enjoy your meal." Uncle Vito nodded. Then he looked at me and narrowed his eyes. "But not too much, capiche?"

An obvious side glance at Gabe made it clear what he was talking about.

"*Bye*, Uncle Vito, Harold—I'll see you at class in a few days."

"He's *really* a character." Gabe chuckled after

the men left. Their bickering and backbiting could be heard three tables away.

"Which one?" I asked, and we both laughed. "Hey, by the way—was that really a blessing on his house? You seemed to know what Uncle Vito said."

"I did." Gabe shook his head slowly. "And no, Fortuna. It most definitely was *not*."

* * *

Well. *This is awkward*, I thought to myself as Gabe and I walked into my shop.

Ollie and Pepper stood to one side, Martin and Jeeves to the other. Azalea sat behind the counter, reading. As I gazed around the room, I tried to do a quick tally of who knew what.

Gabe knew about the urn, but *not* that Jeeves was a vampire *or* about the ghost women.

Pepper knew about the urn and that Jeeves was a vampire, but not about the ghost women.

Well, no one really knew about the ghost women.

Ollie knew about the urn. Maybe he knew about Jeeves...right. He's been with Pepper all morning. Of *course* he now knew about Jeeves. Pepper shoots off her mouth so much she must eat bullets for breakfast.

Martin knew about the urn. And that Jeeves was a vampire.

And Jeeves...

Okay, he *could* know about the ghost women.

Man, my head hurt.

I hate secrets.

"I need to talk to Jeeves," I announced before anyone could say anything.

Martin and Jeeves looked at each other. Something seemed to pass between them, and then Jeeves nodded. With a step forward, he walked toward the back of the room and into the private area behind the counter.

"Hey, before you go—did you find out anything?" Pepper asked, her face hopeful.

Don't you dig up more snakes than you can kill. Miss Bessie's colorful warning blared in my mind. I wanted to tell Pepper all the things Miss Bessie shared with me, but there was one thing I did know that stopped me.

Pepper would tell Gabe. Without a doubt.

And I didn't want to come between family.

"Later," I told her. Then I followed Jeeves through the back and up the stairs.

"Yes?"

"*What* do you know?" I asked more tersely than I intended.

"Is that a *general* question, or did you have

something more specific in mind?" Jeeves responded in a smooth tone. "If it's a general question, we'll be here quite a while."

"You know *exactly* what I mean," I muttered under my breath. "You're a more powerful telepath than I am, and considering your job? I *highly* doubt you've locked yourself down the way I have."

"You are correct, the abilities that aid me in doing my job are not modified in any way. And some of them are quite enhanced," he agreed. "You want to know if I know you are the foundling from thirty-odd years or so ago and if I know that you are hiding the fact that you are originally from this town?"

"Well, that answers *that* question. And what you know Martin knows?"

Jeeves turned away from me and sat down on my couch, making himself comfortable. He extended a hand, inviting me to take a seat on my own chair across from him. Which, even though it annoyed me, I did.

"When you told Pepper I was not a pet?" he asked, shocking me. Pepper and I were completely and *totally* alone when I said that to her. I didn't know whether he witnessed the discussion through some kind of telepathic distance viewing, whether he read it in my mind, in Pepper's mind—but the fact that he knew it *at all* was downright unsettling.

"That's true. I told you before—I'm not some enslaved paranormal under the sway of my master."

"You're not answering the question—"

"I am," Jeeves cut me off gently. "*If* you'll let me."

I closed my mouth and crossed my arms.

"Witches and vampires, we're closer to one another then you would think. You and I are closer to one another than Martin and I are, in a way. Just because he's human."

"So, you *didn't* tell him?"

"I don't tell him everything, no. I am like any other person—I have a job and commitments. There are things I swore to do for Martin, but I am not some wind-up toy that he can use for whatever he wants, no matter the morality. There are also things I may do for his own good that I won't share with him."

I raised my eyebrow, not quite believing that.

Jeeves bristled at my doubt. "I'm *not* an inanimate object. I have my own codes of honor, my own loyalties, my own self-preservation needs."

I scratched my head. "But what does that have to do with—"

"You are a witch," Jeeves told me. "You and I can hurt each other, but *you* can hurt *me* from a distance. Admittedly, I have a mighty knife—but bringing a knife to a gunfight, as the old saying goes?

It's not very effective. If you and I were to face one another," he admitted, clearly uncomfortable, "you would have a significant advantage."

"So?"

"That means even if I didn't like you, even if I *didn't* care about you for Martin's sake, I would *still* respect you as one of the few creatures in this world that can take my immortality from me with a flick of your wrist. *If* you so choose," Jeeves explained. "My goal is to never give you a reason to contemplate that choice."

I rolled my eyes. "Jeeves, I wouldn't know the first *thing* about how to—"

"But you *will*," the handsome vampire responded, leaning forward. "You *have* the power. And once you access it, learn to use it—and you *will*, you know. You will have to if you are to unravel the mystery the Mystic Mother presented you with—"

"The *Mystic Mother?*" I laughed. "Is that like the *Queen Mother?*"

"We're digressing." Jeeves leaned back and stared at me like I was a misbehaving college student disrupting a serious lecture with the giggles. "I imagine who and what I am caught you by surprise, and I understand your questions. You believed, for *whatever* reason,"—said, by the way, in a tone that made *clear* his shock and amusement at my naivete—"that you were the only paranormal in this town. You are not. We are, however, members of the same large tribe. You have my loyalty—"

"Martin has your loyalty—"

"—*unless* I believe keeping *your* trust will violate the trust I have built with Martin."

I tried not to feel irritated. I'd talked to Jeeves twice now and was beginning to realize something. Speaking to the vampire *sort of* answered questions. It also opened up a gigantic, Costco-sized can of other questions.

"I am a complicated man. Vampires *usually* are." He half-smiled as he answered my thoughts.

"So, can I count on you to keep the mystic thing secret?" I asked him point blank.

"For now, of course." Jeeves nodded. "You may also call on me for assistance with it if you wish."

My eyes narrowed. "What do you mean *for now?*"

"I told you," he said as he stood up. "As long as what you do does not pose a threat to Martin, you have my loyalty, confidence, and assistance. If needed."

"And if it does?" I asked against my better judgment.

The vampire's eyes burned with intensity as we stared at one another across the room. There was something mesmerizing about him...as if he was wrapped in a subtle, hypnotic charm. *Maybe he was*, I thought. I didn't know who the witches were that had burrito-wrapped him in magic, and there were so many layers, I couldn't identify it all.

"Let's hope it never comes to that," he finally responded after a loaded silence. "For everyone's sake."

SIXTEEN

Pepper walked into my living room and sat down in the seat Jeeves had vacated just a few minutes before. "So, did you find out *who* took the urn?"

"No, I told you, I was looking into something else," I told her distractedly while chewing on my fingernail. It was a habit from my childhood, a nervous tic that appeared when I was feeling intimidated by my mother, and I hadn't indulged in years.

Over the course of this day, I'd gone from feeling confident in my ability to juggle all the things in Mystic's End competing for my attention to not knowing what issue I should tackle first.

And whether I could.

Should I start combat magic training so I can defend myself against a vampire attack?

Should I learn more about dowsing first so I can find the witch bottles?

Should I go visit Irma at the library and get more history books?

Talk to Ollie about the Holy Grove Church—or hide what I know from him and investigate on my own? I trusted Ollie to a point. But Kane was his father.

What happens if I don't tell Gabe and he discovers I've been hiding all this from him?

And how will I hide the mystic stuff from Pepper? That girl was like a dog with a bone—or Gideon with bacon—when she sniffed out a fact whose existence she didn't know.

But, you know, circling back—a freaking *vampire.* A powerful, mind-reading vampire that answers every commitment he makes with a codicil and an implicit warning. Wrapped in protective magic by mob witches—

"Fortuna!" Pepper shouted.

"Jeez! You don't have to shout!" I pulled my attention back outside myself and refocused on my friend. "Did you say something? I didn't catch it if you did."

"No kidding! I *asked* you if we were going to keep looking into the urn or not?" Pepper asked with exasperation. "We've been working on it for days, and suddenly you seem *completely* uninterested in solving the case. Did you learn what you needed to know about Martin or something?"

I shook my head no, but offered no more than that. I tried to reach back and remember why I had bothered to look into this. So much information was new, so much had changed, that the dinner Martin and I had now felt very far away.

"What on earth's going *on* with you?" She looked me up and down. "What are you not telling me?"

Oh, for goodness sake. Was *she* a telepath now?

Suddenly, I felt tired.

I started the week feeling settled but a little suspicious of the guy courting me. Now, I had to sift through all of this information, and nothing was exactly as I thought it was.

Hellfire, nothing was *remotely* what I believed it to be.

I forced a smile. "It's nothing. I think I'm just tired, you know? And finding out there was another paranormal in town? It just threw me for a loop, that's all."

Pepper continued to look at me suspiciously. "You're a truly *terrible* liar sometimes. Why don't I believe you?"

"Because you're a skeptic by nature. You also don't believe that we landed on the moon."

"Hey, I've got good evidence it was faked, you know. Anyway," Pepper waved a hand dismissively and gave me a broad smile as if all her concern simply dissipated. "Everyone is still downstairs, you know. Are we going to find this urn, or what?"

"I guess so." I nodded. "Though, honestly, I don't feel like we're any closer to figuring out who took it, if anyone, than we were."

"I still think you should just ask the vampire."

"Maybe," I told her noncommittally.

Wait.

The vampire.

The vampire can't be picked up on video.

"You're plotting something." Pepper leaned forward. "I can tell, your forehead gets all wrinkly."

"I think we should do one thing before we ask the vampire."

"What's that?"

"Find out what powers vampires have." I stood up and crossed my arms. "We've been focusing on humans that would steal the urn for money, right? Suddenly, we find out that Martin's guard is a vampire, *and* witches have cast protection on him. Maybe there's a *reason* we're not finding anything on that videotape." I raised my eyebrow. "Get my meaning?"

Pepper's jaw dropped. "You think something *supernatural* might have taken the urn."

"I think that the number of women you said came in and out of Martin's house? That was a *lot* of women. You assumed he was...well, we all know what you assumed," I told her with a wince. "But what if you're wrong? What if these weren't women he was dating? What if they were the witches associated with his family?"

"Hold on. You think Evangeline Laroux is a *witch*?" Pepper's jaw dropped again.

"Look, I didn't say *every* woman had a paranormal reason to be there," I told her in a caustic tone.

"Have you ever been up on the second floor of his house?" Pepper asked, her brows furrowed.

"No. You?"

"Dude, I've never *been* to his house. Like, hardly *anyone* in town has. In fact," she mused aloud, "it's been a bit of a mystery, that house. No parties, no nothing. People assumed when he built this great big showplace of a house with a fancy Chicago architecture firm and outside construction teams—"

"*Wait* a minute, back up. Mystic Construction Co. built the Complex, almost every home in the area, but they *didn't* build Martin's house?" MCC was owned by the Abernathy family, an old-money clan close to Reverend Dexter Kane. I got on the wrong side of them from the get-go when I discovered Hoyt Abernathy and Evangeline Laroux (who, at that time, went by Rowena Clutterbuck) were *not* the upstanding citizens Mystic's End was supposed to believe them to be.

"Yeah, no." Pepper shrugged. "We all just figured he had some specific needs and the money to get 'er done exactly the way he wanted. There wasn't anything odd about the companies he brought in, though. Believe me, I looked—" Suddenly frowning, the reporter turned, dug around in her backpack and pulled out a steno pad. She flipped through pages at rapid speed, scanning every page. "Right, here it is. This wasn't odd *then*, but the company is owned by the Salvatore Family Trust."

"His *father*," I murmured.

"His father," she repeated. "But what does it mean?"

I didn't know. But I needed to find out.

* * *

Pepper and I crouched in the corner behind the bed as Gideon stood guard at the top of the stairs. The third floor was quiet and far away from the others down below.

I couldn't shake the feeling Jeeves knew precisely what I was doing.

And why.

"Okay, *don't* freak out again," I told Pepper as I pulled out the small cauldron. It contained a rainbow-colored block of gel. I whispered a few words, and the block melted. Seconds later, the small container was steaming.

"I'm *not* gonna freak out," Pepper huffed. "Okay, the first time I saw it? Yeah, I freaked out. Totally. Can you blame me? Little tiny man in a cauldron, hand *sticking out*? I mean, come on, Fortuna. If you didn't know any of this was real, wouldn't it freak *you* out?"

"You ran a paranormal blog," I whispered, waving at her to keep her voice down.

"Yeah, well, there's writing about rainbow goo that can teleport stuff, and *seeing* it with a hand sticking out of it."

"Fortuna!" Gunther said happily as the mist slowly coalesced his form. My old friend and former witchy trainer looked happy and relaxed, with a broad smile on his face. "You want me to get Charlotte? She's putting the baby down for his afternoon nap, but I'm sure she'd love to talk to you. It's been a while."

"Can he see me?" Pepper whispered, her eyes wide.

"And hear you, yes," Gunther nodded. "Nice to meet you."

"Are you, like, a leprechaun?" Pepper stared at his four-inch-tall image, leaning on her hands and knees to get a closer look. "Or a fairy? You're *so* small."

Gunther laughed. "We gave Fortuna a mini-cauldron to keep in touch. It can't do full-size visitations. But I assure you, I'm quite normal-sized."

"Wow," Pepper said, poking the hazy air. She yelped as her hand disappeared into the mist.

"*Shut* up!" I hissed at her.

"What the—"

"I'll explain later," I told her, rolling my eyes. She saw a hand come *out* of it. How did she not realize a hand could go *into* it?

Turning back to Gunther, I told him he didn't need to bother Charlotte. "I have kind of an emergency. Vampires. There's a vampire in Mystic's End. He's a really powerful telepath, and even though I'm all self-wrapped in the blocks and protections that Priestess Goodfellow taught me? He's made it clear I'm pretty much an open book to him. Is there *anything* I can do?"

Gunther's face looked concerned, even worried. "This vampire. Is he coming after you?"

"No, we're actually friends. Well, *kind* of." I

shrugged. "But I don't like the idea that anyone can just rummage around in my head and pluck what they want out of it."

"Well, *that's* some irony for you," Pepper snorted.

I glared at her.

"Hold on, Samson's...Ow, stop!" Gunther disappeared from the mist, and a cat head poked out. It solidified, then grew to standard size. Suddenly, Samson and I were staring eye to eye, his head the only visible part of him.

"Samson," I bowed my head. "Nice to see you, cat."

Pepper sat frozen, her eyes wide and her jaw dropped so far Samson could fit his head in it with room to spare if he tried.

"Fortuna," a voice echoed within my mind. "You're looking well. Kept the blonde hair, huh?" The cat sniffed and then frowned. "You have a *dog* familiar? A *dog?*"

"I can *hear* the disembodied cat," Pepper choked.

"Well, *she's* a bright one, isn't she?" Samson said, sniffing with derision as he glared at Pepper. "All the humans in all the world, and you picked *this* one? And *a dog?* Decided to indulge a slumming phase, I suppose?"

"Hey!" Pepper protested hotly.

"Let's focus, please!" I whispered. "Did you stick your head through the mists just to make fun of my life choices, or do you have something you can tell me about vampires?"

The cat's eyes went hazy, and his face tensed. Then he jerked. And he jerked again. With a horrible retching sound, he coughed up a jewel covered in cat hair, bile, and saliva.

"That's *really* gross, Samson." I picked up the small black gem with a tissue and tried to clean it off without hurling. "Why on earth did you have this in your stomach?"

"I'm a *cat*. I have a pocket of otherworld space in my gut where I store things. How *else* am I supposed to get things out of it? This works just fine, *thank* you very much. If you don't approve, feel *free* to give it back." Samson opened his mouth wide, his sharp teeth glinting as he waited.

"What is it?" Pepper whispered.

"Never *you* mind, little human. Run along and let the paranormals talk," Samson told Pepper with a glare so dismissive I felt Pepper wither.

And Pepper *doesn't* wither.

"It must be in contact with your skin for it to work," the cat explained, "but that should stop the vampire from hearing or seeing your thoughts. *Only* while it's next to your skin. Once you remove it? *All* your thoughts and feelings are up for grabs. Even the ones you had while in contact with the stone."

"It only works against vampires?" I asked the cat (while hoping for coverage that was more expansive).

"I can get you more stones if you need them," he said, and then closed his eyes, his face tensing again as his body convulsed.

"No! No, no, no, Samson, this is good," I waved off the offer.

Gideon had crept up behind us and was staring at the cat head. His tail wagged frantically, and he looked...well, if a dog could be *awestruck*, that's how he looked.

Samson looked Gideon up and down. The two stared at one another silently, Samson impassive and Gideon tightly excited, an eager look on his face.

Sighing, Samson shook his head. "I *suppose* you'll *do*," the cat admitted grudgingly.

Gideon beamed, and my jaw dropped.

I just comprehended *what* Samson had said.

Gideon was my *familiar*.

I thought only *cats* were familiars.

"Only cats *should* be familiars," Samson told me with a huff. "Sometimes, wayward witches decide, for whatever reason, cats are just *too* good for them, and they bond with lesser creatures. It's likely a self-esteem issue, I think."

"I didn't *pick* him, though," I told Samson. "I didn't even realize he was a familiar until just now. I got him from the dog track. Just as a pet."

Samson looked patently uninterested as he licked his paw.

"Anyway, if he's my familiar, what do I *do* with him?"

"Well, according to *him*, you feed him bacon." Samson sniffed and glared at Gideon. "A spindly, skinny, goofy dog. What *is* the paranormal world coming to? Anyway, are we done here? I need to take a nap."

"I just have one more question—"

"Too bad. Should have asked it already. I need a nap," Samson said, and his face disappeared.

Pepper, silent for most of this exchange, stared at the cauldron like it was a seething pile of snakes. "What the heck *was* that?" she asked. "*What* did I just experience?"

"That, believe it or not, was a god," I said, picking up the cauldron as the mist dissipated. "Originally, we thought he was just some kind of special familiar. He was Charlotte's and had been the familiar to every ringmaster in her family. When everything went down, we found out he was actually an honest-to-goodness god."

"*That* snarky cat is a *god?*"

"Yep. You have officially met a paranormal god." I nodded. "Congratulations. How was it?"

"Not *quite* as profound as I thought it would be," Pepper said, obviously disappointed that a god would hock up a hairball—*even* if it was gem-filled. "Man, no wonder the world's kind of whacked if *that's* a god."

"I heard that!" Samson boomed from the fading mist.

Gideon, however, looked emotionally and spiritually moved by the entire experience. He sat erect and alert, his head up, and his eyes shining. He looked...proud.

As if he had just won the biggest race of his life.

SEVENTEEN

Pepper immediately made a beeline for Ollie, who was seated at the newsstand table on the right side of the store. I could see Gabe and Martin engaged in a tense discussion on the other side of the room as I headed over to the counter.

"What's that about?" I whispered to Azalea, dropping down behind the counter, hitching my chin toward the men.

"You," she whispered back. "Well, initially, anyway. They've been talking for a really long time, and I think it's about more than *just* you now."

I popped back up to find Jeeves staring at me, an expression of bemused frustration on his face.

I smiled.

Before Pepper and I had rejoined the crime convention going on in my art store, I had slipped the cat rock into my bra and tucked it underneath my breast. It was the only place I could think of to keep it. With it snugly sandwiched between my torso and the generous gifts I inherited from my mysterious birth mother, it was secure and in constant contact with skin. Later, I'd create something more secure and permanent, but for now?

Boob storage would do.

An image of a pulsing heart appeared in my mind at almost the same time pressure pushed against my leg. Glancing down, I found Gideon staring up at me, his mouth slightly open as if in a smile.

"Hey, boy," I told him softly and crouched down again behind the counter. A calm feeling came over me as I touched him, and it made me wonder if that feeling was some sort of familiar thing. How did Gideon even become my familiar, anyway? Was he born to be one, and I happened to come along? Or did he become one *because* he was destined to be mine?

Gideon licked my face happily, and I shrugged off all the questions.

In the end, it didn't matter.

"You're a good boy, Gideon." In response, he

pressed his barrel chest against me until I hugged the dog, eliciting a friendly snort mixed with a sigh of contentment. "We'll figure out this whole familiar thing as soon as I figure out what happened to that urn," I whispered. "And you know what? I think I'm closer."

"Do you?" a voice asked politely from above. I looked up.

Jeeves was watching me intently.

I wondered if Samson could hock up a stone that would guard against vampires with exceptional hearing. At least they were small. I could fit ten, maybe even twenty, rocks in my bra.

Though it probably wouldn't be very comfortable.

"Pepper and I need to go back to Martin's," I told him. Giving Gideon one last scratch behind the ears, I stood up and faced the vampire. "But first, maybe you can answer something for me. Since you're in charge of security and all."

Jeeves' eyes narrowed, and his body tensed. Boy, he looked frustrated. The gem Samson gave me must be working, and Jeeves wasn't precisely thrilled it was. "Sure, ask away," he answered finally.

"Did you give us all the footage you have for Martin's house?"

"Yes, every bit of it. That's what Martin directed me to do."

"Are there any rooms that don't have cameras?"

"The staff bedrooms and bathrooms, of course," he answered quickly.

Too quickly.

"Hey, Ollie," I called. Jeeves and I continued to look into one another's eyes. "How many rooms are off of the second hallway? Based on that hallway footage, I mean. How many doors?"

I saw a flicker of concern in the vampire's eyes.

"Six," Ollie called out.

"How many rooms can you account for that have footage?"

A pause. "None."

"So, Jerome has a bedroom. Adelaide. That's two. Probably a bathroom. That's three," I said as I ticked off the rooms on my hand. "I assume *you* have a room since the sun isn't an issue for you, so that's four. Martin has a bedroom, so that's five. His office is on the first floor, so what's the purpose of the sixth room?"

The storefront was suddenly quiet.

Jeeves refused to turn around and look at Martin, but I could *see* it in his face. He wanted to. He wanted to *so badly* that it appeared painful for him to hold my gaze. The perfectly plucked vampire eyebrow rose in amusement, and it hit me that Jeeves was deriving a perverse sort of pleasure at being challenged by my words. Words he *should* be able to see behind but which, quite suddenly, he could not.

"Well?" I asked again.

Nothing.

"Man, it just got *tense* up in here," Pepper observed.

"So, this is weird," Ollie said calmly. I heard the computer keys clacking away. And more keys. And more keys. "Yeah, definitely odd. There are *no* building plans on file for that house. Nothing. That's not just weird, that's unheard of. You can't get a building permit for a house without blueprints on file."

"Well, not in a *normal* town," Pepper added. "Here? Grease the right palms, you can get anything done. And you do have buckets of grease, Martin."

I glanced over at Martin.

Nothing.

Well, not *nothing*.

He was sharing a glance with Gabe.

A knowing glance.

* * *

"I've *had* it, you know?" I told Pepper as she drove toward Martin's mysterious mansion on the hill. "I've *had* drama in my life. First, my mother and then after I left, the circuses. Paranormal wars. I moved here to get away from all that."

"I know," Pepper answered distractedly.

"I wanted to move here, open an art studio, paint pretty things. I wanted a simple life. A quiet life," I complained as the scenery whizzed by. "And what do I get? Slapped by an old woman and turned into some magical symbol of freedom. Chased after by a mafia boss's son who has more secrets than the CIA, while being harassed by the drunken daughter of the town Sheriff."

"I know," she said again.

"And now, a vampire that forces me to wear a stone under my boob just to have private thoughts in my own head!" I told her in exasperation.

"Yeah, you've got it *so* bad," Pepper murmured.

I looked at her sharply. "That didn't sound sincere at all."

"Wow, you must be psychic or something," she responded wryly.

"What's *got* you in a mood?"

"You can be a little tough to understand at times."

"Me?" I asked, surprised. "I'm an open book."

Pepper laughed so hard I thought she would

simultaneously run the car off the road and choke to death doing it. "Yeah, *sure*," she snorted as the laughter came down to a simmer. "You're an open book. Of *course* you are."

"It's not *that* funny," I muttered.

"Actually, you know what? You're right," Pepper said, a sympathetic echo creeping into her voice. "It's *not* really funny. Fortuna, look. I'm not trying to be judgmental. I'm the last person that would pass judgment."

I snorted. "Now, *that's* funny."

"A *god* sought you out this morning, gave you something to protect yourself. A book thrust itself out of the earth to give itself to you. And your reaction...I mean, it was like you were afraid you were plowing too close to the cotton."

I blinked. "I have *no* idea what that means."

"It's an expression. It means you're too cautious."

"Why not just say that?"

"You *do* know you moved to the South, right?" Pepper asked me.

"*Why* does everyone keep asking me that? Look, Pepper—"

"No. *You* listen to me for a change," my friend responded with uncharacteristic seriousness. "I love you. You're one of the first friends I've ever made that's as weird as me. And I don't want to offend you, I really don't. But girl, you got some *issues*."

"Um. Thanks?"

"You have these incredible powers. I mean, *incredible* powers. You were *born* special, Fortuna. All these miraculous things happen around you. And then the circus and your friends giving you all this money to start the shop. I mean...wow, right? People should be so lucky! But whenever these incredible things happen to you, it always seems like you're one step away from it, watching it all from the outside."

I frowned.

"You don't let any of it make you *happy*. You don't seem like you appreciate any of it. You act like it's a burden you *wish* you didn't have. And as someone who would cut off her right arm to have half the powers you have, I don't understand it at all. And, well," Pepper admitted as she glanced quickly at me. "It kind of annoys me. A little."

My jaw dropped. "I *annoy* you?"

"Don't say that like it comes as such a shock. I get annoyed. By you. Sometimes. It seems...I don't know, ungrateful. A little. How you don't notice what you have."

I played back some of the scenes she referenced in my head, readying myself to argue back. But as they played over in my mind, I had to admit she had a point. I wasn't precisely...well, to be blunt, I was kind of cold. A little.

I always saw it as formidable. Stoic.

But maybe it wasn't.

I knew where it came from. My mother hadn't so much as raised me as *trained* me.

Don't act excited about wealth, dear. It's gauche.

Don't wear too much makeup, dear. You look like a trollop.

Don't wear those pants, dear. You look like a man.

Don't wear that dress, dear. You're not shapely enough.

The most I could hope for as a child was that she would say *nothing*.

At least, until my psychic ability manifested itself. Then, the most I could hope for was that my mother's attention would be drawn elsewhere, so I couldn't hear what she *honestly* thought of me in her mind.

That stupid little foundling. I wish she would stop staring at me. It's creepy.

Out of all the children we could have adopted, how did I get stuck with this imbecile?

My god, her hair. It's like she's descended from peasant stock.

Instinctively, I reached up and touched my hair, felt its softness.

"Are you mad at me now?" Pepper asked. "I didn't say it to hurt you."

"I know you didn't." I sighed and dropped my hand. "It's not about being ungrateful. Really, it's not. When I was younger, my mother just...she hated displays of anything. Happiness, sadness, fear. It didn't matter. It was almost like I was supposed to be nothing more than a prop."

"That's horrible."

"It was all I knew, you know? And the only way I learned how to be." I shrugged and stared out the window. "I'm in my thirties, and I'm still trying to figure out who I am in a lot of ways."

"You and everyone else." Pepper glanced at me and smiled.

"Thanks for saying something," I told her sincerely. "I need to think about this."

"Any time." She nodded once and fell silent.

* * *

And I did too, for the rest of the drive. Which was about five minutes.

Then I shoved it back in my internal file folder. Behind everything else I was dealing with.

"How the *heck* did they get ahead of us?" Pepper asked as we pulled up to the house. Martin and Jeeves stood waiting for us. Gabe and Ollie were just a minute behind us.

"Maybe they have a secret entrance or something," I told her.

I opened the passenger side door and got out, joining the vampire and the mafia prince on the walkway. "You sure you're okay with this?" I asked Martin.

Martin and Jeeves looked at one another.

"I asked *you* to help me," he responded without taking his eyes from his guard. "I agreed to let you follow the trail wherever it would lead. I didn't expect you would involve all of *them,*" Martin waved at Pepper, Gabe, and Ollie, "but I *should* have. I should have known. It was a miscalculation on my part, to be sure. But it was one *I* made, and here we are. Now, if I don't allow this, you'll assume I'm hiding something from you."

"You *are* hiding something from me. You could have explained all this, or tried to, back at my shop. You didn't. But you do have a point—you didn't really agree to let everyone else do this, too," I told Martin. "You don't have to agree to this."

"If I ask all of you to not go into my home, not look upstairs, not open that door, will you ever trust me again?" Martin asked me, finally meeting my eyes. "Does our relationship, even our friendship, have a *hope* of surviving this week if I don't submit to this?"

"I don't know."

I hated saying it, but it was the truth.

I didn't.

"Let's do this, then." Martin turned and headed for the house.

EIGHTEEN

"Miss Fortuna!" Adelaide, Martin's housekeeper and cook, greeted me first with a smile, and then a frown as she spotted the small crowd of people following me in. "Sir?" the older woman gasped to her employer, alarmed. Her eyes frantically skipped from person to person as she scrutinized the train of people barreling into her home.

"They just want to see the second floor, Addie," Martin told her without turning around. "It's fine. Just let them do what they have to do."

"Is this all about that silly urn, then?" Addie asked, her fingers pulling on a dishrag she clutched in her hands. "Can't you just get another one,

Martin? All this fuss over a piece of pottery, I just can't see it." Her round face flushed red.

"Your housekeeper's got a point, Martin," Pepper said as we ascended the stairs. "You've got buckets of money. The urn's worth only a quarter of a million. I mean, that's a lot to me, but to you? I bet you have some bottles of wine worth more than that."

"There's only been *one* bottle of wine sold worth more than that urn," Martin told her. "And no, I was not the one that bought it."

The stairs were steep and curved. Like the monotone downstairs, the polished white marble gleamed with little color splashed anywhere to break up the changelessness.

That's probably why I was so surprised when we arrived on the second floor to find a bright red door at the end of the hallway.

"Oh, you've *got* to be kidding me," Gabe murmured under his breath.

"What?" I asked him.

"I saw that movie," he responded, rolling his eyes. "Way cheesier than I expected, Salvi."

Martin glared at him.

"There's no way," Pepper exclaimed, her eyes blazing with curiosity as a sly grin crept across her face. "Your boyfriend's *super* kinky, Fortuna. Has he pulled out a contract yet? I'm betting he's going to pull out a contract."

"What are you talking about?" I asked her, confused.

"We need to have a girls' movie night. I swear, it's like you've been in another dimension…Oh. Right. Never mind."

"Would you people *stop* it!" Martin gritted his teeth and dug around in his pocket, cursing to himself when he didn't find what he was looking for. Jeeves casually stepped in front of him, pulled out a set of keys, and turned to Martin with an intense look. The millionaire sighed and nodded. "Thanks."

"Of course." Jeeves nodded and placed a hand on his shoulder. "Are you sure you want to do this, friend? You don't have to. You know what it means. You know *I* am in favor of it, but I want you to be sure." Martin ground his jaw as the two stared at one another. Finally, he nodded to the vampire. "If you're sure. Just remember. Some things cannot be unseen."

"But *some* can," Martin said, glancing at everyone standing behind me.

"Yes, that's true. Some can."

Suddenly, I was nervous, and I wished I'd brought Samson. I felt like I was standing on a precipice about to jump, and I didn't know what I was jumping into or where the bottom was.

"Hey, look," I said, stepping forward and staring up into Martin's face. "If you don't want to let us in the red room, you don't have to. This may have nothing to do with the urn at all, anyway, right? Pepper's not wrong. You *can* afford to replace it. We can just stop looking if you don't care about finding it."

Martin and I stared at one another, the hallway silent. Waiting.

* * *

"I took it!" Adelaide shouted as she pushed her way through the hallway and stood in front of the door. Her arms were outstretched, her rotund body blocking our entry. "Mr. Salvi, sir, I'm terribly sorry. I broke it while cleaning it! Buried the pieces in the backyard. I don't know where. Don't remember. But I did it. It was me. It was me, sir." She shoved her wrists out toward Gabe. "You can arrest me now. I did it. No need to go in."

"Addie, you leave Mr. Salvi and his friends to their business," Jerome Watson, Martin's butler, admonished Addie in a soothing voice as he picked past us and attempted to pull the woman away from the door. "You didn't break the urn. Come now."

"I did it! I *did* so! No need to go into the room now!" Addie yanked her arm away from Jerome and threw herself back against the wooden door with a thud. "No one needs to look in the room anymore, Mr. Watson. Jeeves, *you* tell them I did it. You can read my mind, can't you?"

"Go into the *room*?" Jerome asked, shocked. The butler whirled gracefully toward Martin and stared at him. "You mean to let *these people* in *that room*? Are you *daft*?"

Pepper and Gabe observed the three while Ollie leaned against the wall, a half-smile on his face, as he gazed on the scene like he was watching a very entertaining movie.

Martin looked angry. "Jerome, calm down."

"Tell them, Jeeves!" Addie shouted. "You tell them I'm telling the truth!"

"Adelaide," Jeeves sighed. "I can't say that."

"You can! You *tell* them! You tell them I did it, and then they can *go*, and no one has to look! They know what you are, don't they?" Addie said as she cast her eyes wildly about the hallway. "They know that, right? They know what you can do, then. If you tell them, they'll *believe* me!"

"I *told* you to leave that woman alone," Jerome snapped at Martin. It was utterly disrespectful and *sounded nothing* like a servant addressing his employer. My eyes narrowed as I looked at each one of Martin's employees carefully. Jeeves calm. Addie panicked. Jerome angry. "Now look what you've done. Why not just get a sword off the wall and let poor Addie *throw* herself on it? Do you ever get tired of people paying for your irresponsible choices, young man?"

Just as Martin was about to answer, Jeeves sighed and stepped toward Gabe so quickly my eyes could barely follow. I felt the swift movement more than saw it.

The vampire gazed into his eyes for a few seconds, and the detective crumpled gently to the floor. Before I could react, Jeeves quickly stared into the eyes of Pepper, then Ollie. Within fifteen seconds, my friends curled around my feet, sleeping peacefully.

"*What* did you do to them?" I asked, shocked.

"What I cannot do to you, unfortunately," Jeeves answered as he walked back to stand behind Martin. "Addie, let Fortuna go in the room."

"But I—"

"Adelaide," Jeeves turned and held out his arm. "Trust me. Let Fortuna enter the room."

I swallowed and wrapped my arms around myself.

I didn't know if I *wanted* to go in the room anymore.

"This *isn't* about an urn, is it?" I asked Jeeves.

"No," Martin said.

"Yes," Jeeves said and looked at Martin. "It is. I'll explain once we're inside."

Martin's chest rose and fell with rapid breaths, and he looked unsure of himself. Then he turned and said, "I trust him. I promise."

"Well, I'm glad *you* trust him." I gave a bitter laugh. "Because as I stand here trying to take all this in, my friends collapsed in a heap at my feet, *your* trust in the vampire makes me feel a whole lot better. Really." Martin gazed back and me, but didn't respond.

I turned my attention back to the red door, concentrating. I got no sense of it.

Damn it.

My stomach in knots, I took down shield after shield, block after block. Every magical containment I wrapped myself in came off like many layers of sheer clothing, energy sliding down to the floor, and dissipating among my sleeping friends.

Pepper snored.

I rolled my shoulders, planted my feet, and reached out psychically toward the door. Heavy magical energies reached back as if in greeting.

"Whoa." I let out a harsh breath.

"It'll be okay," Martin whispered. "I would

never let anything happen to you. You have to know that."

"Oh, for goodness's sake." Jerome leveled a warning glare at Martin that none of us missed. "This never should have come to pass. Never. I warned you. I *warned* you. If your father found out about this, Martin—"

"That's enough." Jeeves stared at the butler, his eyes dangerously dark.

Jerome studied the vampire—taking great care not to meet his eyes.

"Just tell me. What is behind the magic door?" I asked no one in particular.

"Nothing!" Jerome shouted, whirling on me. "None of this concerns you at all, young woman, so it's best if you just take your friends, leave, and never return! Martin never should have—"

Jerome mistakenly glanced at Jeeves for a moment, *just* a moment, and their eyes met for a split-second. That was all it took. With a sigh, the butler slid against the wall and drifted gently to the ground. He snored louder than Pepper.

"Oh, why'd you go and do that, Mr. Jeeves?" Addie complained. "We're all going to get in trouble!"

"It'll be fine," the vampire assured her.

"In trouble? How?" I asked the woman.

Her mouth opened and then closed. Opened and closed. She looked like a fish gasping for air.

"Is *someone* going to tell me what's going on?" I asked with exasperation.

"We will," Jeeves said, pointing toward the red door. "Once you open it."

"If you want it opened so badly, why don't *you* open it?"

"Because then he won't know if you *can* open it, Fortuna." Martin sighed and rubbed his eyes with his hands. "And if you *can't* open it, it would be dangerous for us to tell you anything about what's behind that door."

"Trust us, just for a moment. Just long enough to open the door," Jeeves said. "All your questions will be answered once you step through it."

"I feel like a lot of horror movies that start this way," I muttered.

I stared at the door.

And then I opened it.

* * *

"Whoa."

The room was something out of a fantasy movie. Dark gray stone lined the walls as if the room itself had been transported from a castle and shoved within the modern mansion. Shelves of bottles that looked like they came straight out of a magical apothecary. A gigantic cauldron sat on one end of the room, bubbling rainbow-colored mist...

Wait a minute.

"Are *you* a witch?" I asked Martin. "Because this screams—and I mean *screams*—witch room. I know what that is," I told him, pointing to the cauldron. "And if you're human, you can't even *use* it without a witch activating it!"

"He can't, that's true," Addie said as she walked toward me. "But I can."

"*You're* a witch?"

The woman nodded. "Not a full one, but yes."

"What's Jerome?" I asked.

"A jerk," Addie snapped.

"He's human, Fortuna," Jeeves explained, his poker-face still intact. "Jerome works for Martin's father. To keep an eye on him. Tell her, Martin," Jeeves said gently to his friend. "Tell her why you're here in Mystic's End."

A vein popped out on Martin's neck as he stared back at the vampire.

"Martin?" I asked.

"This is ridiculous!" he shouted, glaring at all three of us. He paced ...

...and that's when I spotted them.

On the shelf.

Witch bottles.

"Three witch bottles," I whispered. "Those are *witch bottles*." They were small and nondescript. Were you gazing at the room and its strange and brightly colored contents, you'd miss them. They looked old and were caked in dirt as if they had been dug up. They did not stand out unless you knew what they were. "*Where* did you get them?"

"How do *you* know what they are?" Jeeves asked me. His eyes, however, were locked with Martin's, an I-told-you so expression on his face.

"Uh-uh, buddy, it's time for *you* to answer questions. I didn't come here for an interview, and you both promised you'd explain once we were in here. I passed your test. We're in here. So, you tell *me*. Where did you get those bottles?"

"I found them," Adelaide told me. I turned to face the kindly woman. "I scried and was able to find three. I know there's more. I can *feel* them!" The old woman's voice suddenly raged, and anger flew off her like a wave. "But I cannot break them and release the souls bound within them." Tears welled up in her eyes, and she sniffed loudly. "I have tried. I am just not strong enough. Maybe when I was a younger witch, I could have...but no. I can't anymore."

I instinctively stepped toward the woman to comfort her, but thought better of it and stopped where I was. I still had no clear picture of what was going on here. "How did you know there were souls locked in there?"

She leaned back and looked at the ceiling, her eyes angst-filled. "My sister. My sister is here, somewhere, in the town. Maybe she's on that shelf," Adelaide waved at the bottles. "Maybe she's still beneath the earth. Maybe I'll *never* find her." The housekeeper sobbed so hard that she gasped for breath.

I waited for Jeeves or Martin to comfort the old woman and then rolled my eyes when they didn't. Men.

I walked over to the short woman and wrapped her in my arms, pushing energy of hope and love around the weeping Adelaide. Slowly, she relaxed in my arms and wiped the snot from her face with the rag she had never loosened her grip on.

"You're a good girl." She nodded as she pulled away.

"Can you help Aunt Addie?" Martin asked, his voice hopeful.

Aunt Addie?

I turned and stared at him. "What do you mean, *Aunt* Addie?"

Martin stared, his head dropping in what looked like grief.

"The bound soul she seeks is Martin's mother," Jeeves explained.

NINETEEN

Standing in the witch room, Martin didn't look like a powerful titan of commerce. He looked like a boy caught someplace he shouldn't be. The millionaire's face twisted in pain, anger, and frustration as he looked from Jeeves to Addie.

"I thought you told me you were from *Las Vegas?*" I asked Martin.

"I am," he responded with as much of a smile as he could fake under the circumstances.

"Then how is your mother—" I stopped before I said too much.

Clearly, Jeeves had some idea that I was essential to their quest to free Martin's mom from her witch bottle (if she was even in one), but my trust in this group was at an *all-time* low. It was also clear *someone* standing in this room knew *precisely* where the urn was, and its disappearance had been nothing more than a ruse to get me in this room.

But *whose* manipulation was it? Martin's? Addie's?

I turned and gave Jeeves a sideways look.

"Martin's mother left Mystic's End as a young woman. She dreamed of becoming a showgirl," the vampire explained. "Eventually, she achieved this. Martin's father owned the casino that hosted the show she starred in. They fell in love and married."

"Then *why* do you think your mother is trapped in a witch bottle in Mystic's End?" I asked Martin directly.

"Anna and I came here after I got interested in genealogy," Addie answered for her nephew. "The Otto's history in this town went way back, all the way back to the beginning. We wanted to see it."

"My mother got into an argument with the Mayor at the time," Martin said quietly. "Apparently, there was family land, a good-sized parcel, on the east end of Mystic's End. The town went through the process of having it declared abandoned, and then the state used it for the prison complex."

"Anna wasn't happy about *that*," Addie said, smiling as her eyes grew wet with tears. "She threatened to get my brother-in-law's lawyers to challenge what they'd done, said they had stolen her family's legacy. Told them she would have the whole prison moved before she was done, brick by brick if she had to. My sister was a spitfire."

"Why was some parcel of land in the backwoods of Arkansas so important to her?" I looked around in confusion. "It sounds like she was a wealthy woman. She could have purchased land in the town if she wanted. What's so important about *that* land?"

"Nothing important about it." Addie shrugged. "Anna just didn't like what they'd done. It wasn't fair, and Anna valued fairness above anything else."

"Fairness?" I asked, shocked. "I'm sorry, I don't mean to be disrespectful, but she married a mafia boss, didn't she? How much could she value *fairness*, really?"

Addie looked hurt by my comment. "Love lets people overlook a lot of things, Miss Fortuna. It doesn't change who *they* are."

"I think we're getting off track here," Jeeves said as he stepped forward, his mouth compressed in a tight line. "To make a long story short, Anna challenged the town leaders. Before Addie and Anna could contact Marty, Martin's father, Anna was found in the woods. The authorities claimed she tripped and hit her head on a rock."

Just like Tom Wilson.

How many people tripped in the woods and died in this town?

"When was this?"

"A little over ten years ago," Addie replied.

"Just before you came here and started plans to build the track," I said to Martin. He nodded. "You came here because your mother died here?"

"I did."

"Why?"

"Because my mother was part witch," Martin explained as he lowered his head. A moment later, he raised his eyes. "And before you ask, no, I don't have any powers. Not that I know of, anyway. Maybe I'm able to rely on my instincts a little more than most. But nothing like you or my aunt."

"We could talk to the dead, you see," Addie explained. "Had always done it in my family. When anyone passes, we always get a visit to say goodbye. But this time, even though I was *here?* Anna never came to me. And she *promised* me she would."

"The family knew something happened to Anna's very soul," Jeeves explained. "The witches Marty Salvatore had on staff confirmed they couldn't reach her. I could not, either. Her spirit never seemed to leave this town, at least according to those spectral family members we could contact."

"I stayed," Addie said. "And I was able to find out some things. Irma, in the library, was a great help. I think that Anna made someone important, someone with magic, really angry. And I think they trapped her here as punishment. She's stuck in a bottle somewhere. I just know it."

I glanced again at the three bottles on the shelf and shuddered.

Anna Salvatore wasn't even a resident of Mystic's End. She came back to learn her origins and may have wound up trapped in a bottle for making the wrong man angry. How strong *was* this curse supposedly laid upon the town? And why were so many people caught in its web?

"Have you tried to break the bottles you found?" I asked Addie.

"In every way I can think of," Addie replied, her lips barely moving. It was as if her failure was just too painful to speak out. "Even if Anna's not in there, *someone* is. That much I can tell. Someone's in there. And it grieves me to know it."

"I agree," Jeeves added. "I can sense them."

It could be Anna or Gabe's mother, Mary. Or any of twenty-five other women.

"What do you want from me?" I asked bluntly.

"We hoped, with your history, that you could free the souls in the bottles," Jeeves told me. "This room is enchanted so that only those that mean

Martin no ill will, only those with high levels of magic, can open it. We had to be sure before telling you. You understand, I hope."

"You couldn't have just *asked* me to open the door?" I asked, with undisguised aggravation.

No one answered.

As per usual with Mystic's End, the more I knew, the less I understood.

* * *

I took my leave to get some air.
Standing alone on the back veranda of Martin's house overlooking Mystic's End, I could see everything. The whole town laid out in front of me.

To the east, I could see the dark and ominous walls of Arcadia Prison nestled among the woodlands. To the west, the lights of the greyhound track could be clearly seen. Straight south, I knew the Holy Grove Church was almost directly across from me. Encircled between, the weird town of Mystic's End.

Like the quarters of a witches' circle.

With my shop and home in the center.

I had never told Martin outright about my being *the mystic*. From the conversation inside the witch room, it didn't sound like they knew. Though I found it hard to believe that Jeeves *didn't* know—considering the months he had open access to my mind.

So many secrets.

"How did such a ridiculous little town in Arcadia County, Arkansas, become such a hotbed of paranormal activity?" I murmured to myself as the wind whipped at my shirt and tossed my hair. "Wasn't this supposed to be my *normal* life?"

"Is this a conversation of one?" Jeeves asked quietly.

I hadn't even heard the back door open. That vampire was as silent as death.

Only death wasn't silent.

Not in my world.

"You took the urn, didn't you?" I asked him without turning around. "You're the only one that wouldn't show up on the camera. You're the only one that could have moved fast enough to make the replacement in between blinks of the security camera's shutter. *You* stole it. You stole it to get me here and into that room."

"Yes." His tone was unapologetic.

"Does Martin know you took it?"

"No."

"You *manipulated* him," I told him as I crossed my arms and breathed in the fresh air deeply. "You manipulated him, and you manipulated me to get us where you wanted us."

"Yes."

I sucked in the air again and tried to avoid blowing my stack. I could feel the resentment building in my gut, and anger that Jeeves had toyed with me. Fury he had played with my life.

"You're angry," he said simply.

"Of *course* I'm angry," I said as I turned to face him. "I *want* to be able to trust you and Martin, Jeeves, but I have to tell you. You're not making that easy."

"I did what I had to do," Jeeves responded simply. His face was smooth, handsome, and those intense eyes seemed to bore right into me. "You would not have trusted me if I shared what you are with Martin. He would not have trusted me if I kept it from him for long, or if I told you why he was here. Once you found the book, you put me in a difficult position."

The nerve of this guy. "*I* put *you* in a difficult position?"

"One you would have known of," he said with a smirk, "had you simply chosen to *use* your powers, Fortuna. You have no problem using powers to block me from your mind. You could have discovered this. Due to that, I feel no regret about manipulating someone who could have easily discovered the truth—had she simply chosen to."

My eyes narrowed. "And lying to Martin?"

"I never lied to him. I simply didn't volunteer the truth. I followed the rules set upon me." Jeeves shrugged. "But this isn't about Martin and me. This is about you. You followed your own rules, and because of that, I was able to manipulate you. You might wish to think about that, Fortuna."

My pulse shot up, and I felt suddenly short of breath. "You're a real piece of work, you know that?"

"Thank you." The vampire didn't look offended.

"That wasn't a compliment!" I shot back.

"I'm sorry you feel that way."

He so *wasn't* sorry. Who did this guy think he was? I was trying to respect people's privacy! To be a good person! Something Jeeves clearly didn't know the *first* thing about.

And what's more, Jeeves knew that my choice to not deal with Martin had been taken away completely. They had three of the bottles sitting up in their witch room. I needed those bottles, and once I tried to break them, they would know whether I could help them.

I stopped short and stared at him.

Holy crap.

That was it.

That had been Jeeves' intention all along.

Stupid vampire.

He was good. I had to give him that.

* * *

"I'm not ready to talk to any of you about anything right now," I said as I walked back into the house. Addie and Martin sat at the bar, whispering —a conversation that ended as soon as I walked in. "I need to check out your story and think about this."

"I understand," Martin said.

"Are my friends still sleeping in your hallway?" I asked him.

He nodded.

"Can you wake them up?"

Martin looked at Jeeves, and Jeeves nodded.

"We need to get out of here," I told him. "There's someone I need to talk to about all this."

As Jeeves ascended the stairs to wake the hallway full of sleeping humans, Martin stared at me. After what felt like an eternity, he spoke. "I wanted to tell you. I just didn't know if it was safe. For my mother, *or* for you."

"I said I don't want to talk about it."

Martin glanced over at Addie, then back. He nodded.

"I do have a couple of questions, though, just to clarify," I said. "The women that came in and out of this house. They were witches helping Addie, weren't they? They traveled here through the cauldron," I guessed.

"Most of them, yes." Martin nodded.

"And how does your father feel about what you're doing here?"

"Dad thinks that Mom is gone, and he doesn't believe what Addie believes." Martin shifted uncomfortably. "But he's not from here, and he won't talk about it with me. I think it's too painful for him to think that Mom's been trapped in a bottle somewhere in the...He just doesn't talk about it much with me. But he knows why we're here."

"And the greyhound track? What's the purpose of that?"

"I needed a reason to be in this town, and something that would allow me to rise to the top of it quickly," he told me. "Nothing opens doors like money and power."

Yuck. Not wrong. But yuck.

"And the last question," I said, leaning forward. "Are *you* okay with the fact that Jeeves just manipulated this whole song and dance without our consent? That he faked a theft just to throw us together in hopes I'd dig this up on my own?" Martin's eyes widened in surprise. "He hadn't told you yet?"

"No, I...No. No, he didn't." Martin's face looked drawn and exhausted, and for a moment, I felt sorry for him. Martin glanced over his shoulder at Addie, who was looking down at the hands in her lap. She didn't look up. "Look, I'm sorry," he said as he turned back. "I would never have got you involved if I'd known. I...Fortuna, I'm so sorry."

"Save it," I snapped, though I couldn't understand why I was angry at him. Jeeves said flat out that Martin had no idea what he'd done.

Yet, somehow, it felt like Martin's fault.

"What are you going to tell your friends?" Martin whispered as we heard the hallway sleepers clunking down the marble stairs.

"I have no idea," I snapped again. "Not like the truth gets very far in this town, right?"

TWENTY

The urge to wash my eyes out with soap was strong.

"You could have *knocked*, dear," Miss Bessie said as she pulled her shirt over her head. Harold Whatnow frantically wiped at his grizzled face with a tissue, his cheeks pink with embarrassment. His attempts to remove the lipstick from his face only resulted in bigger smears. "Sometimes, I'm otherwise occupied."

"I can see that," I answered from the doorway. "Should I come back?"

"We weren't doin' nothin'!" Harold barked at me.

"Be careful, Harold. I *could* take that as an insult," Miss Bessie warned him. "Why don't you give Fortuna and me some privacy, dear? You and I can finish our *talk* after she leaves."

"We weren't doin' nothin'," Harold grumbled, He squeezed by me on his way out of Miss Bessie's private room at Mystic Memories. He stopped and gave me a direct look. "You hear? Nothin'."

"I hear you, Harold," I answered, wide-eyed.

Harold turned and made his way into the hallway.

"Close the door, dear." Miss Bessie waved me in. "You look like you've had one heck of a day. Come, sit, tell me all about it."

As I explained all that I'd discovered and all that I'd seen, Miss Bessie paid more attention. At the revelation that Martin's mother was affected by the curse and somehow related to the original Mystic's End coven, her jaw dropped.

"Well, I didn't see *that* coming," the old woman murmured. "Are Gabe, Ollie, and Pepper all right?"

"They didn't even seem to remember they'd been put to sleep. In fact, they seemed to not remember why we were at the house at all," I told her. Miss Bessie looked surprised. "I think I need to study vampire powers. I don't know how Jeeves did it, but the fact that he *did* do it is just crazy. You really didn't have any idea that Addie was a partial witch?"

"Well, dear, a *lot* of people in this town have

some witch blood," she responded hastily. "It's just not something you notice after a while. Most of it's so watered down they have to search for their own instinct with two hands and a flashlight. I'm sure *most* of them have no idea. And I've never met Addie."

"So, what do I do?" I asked her.

Miss Bessie gave me a long look. "What are you asking *me* for?"

"I thought you were supposed to be my mystic guide or guru or something?" I stared back expectantly.

"You want *my* advice on something I didn't even know? They've been here almost ten years with witches traipsing in and out of his house like it was the fishnet hose sale counter at a Halloween store. Clearly, the *visus* didn't clue me into anything. So, either I was too old to buy a clue, or I wasn't *meant* to know about them."

"Meant by *who*?" I asked her. "You keep saying things that make it sound like something or someone is controlling this whole thing."

"Well, someone or something is, of course."

"Who?"

The old woman shrugged. "How would I know? The women. Nature. I don't know."

"You know, you've switched from this all-knowing old wise woman to someone who doesn't know squat *awfully* fast."

"Fortuna Delphi, has it not occurred to you that you've discovered three bottles, and a witch that can find them, just *days* after being told they even exist?" Miss Bessie asked me, her bony finger waving in my direction. "I knew about them for years, I never found a *single* witch bottle. Not one."

I felt like I had a dozen things to say, but I said nothing. Miss Bessie was right. It *hadn't* occurred to me how oddly timed that was, or that I had stumbled into something accidentally she had searched her whole life to find. "You're right," I admitted finally. "I didn't think of that."

"I don't begrudge you your luck, 'Tuna—"

"Don't call me 'Tuna."

"—but the fact is our side's been playing with a decaying deck of cards for generations. The only thing the slap passes," Miss Bessie said as she leaned forward, "is the *visus*, and the ability to free the imprisoned witches. Oh, sure, we get *some* of our witch powers boosted, probably because of our tie to the bottles and the witches they hold. But you can only do so much with what's there, you hear? I didn't *have* much there," Miss Bessie shrugged. "*You* started out with a brand new deck of cards."

"If all it takes is angering one of the men descended from that invading group to bring down the curse on someone's head, how are *you* not stuck in a bottle?" I asked her.

"The slap passing on the mystic power *also* gives us protection," Miss Bessie told me quietly. "It ensures that there's always one woman able to challenge the curse and one woman that can *maybe* break it. I failed." The old woman frowned. "And it used to flay my heart, especially after my Mary." Miss Bessie's eyes filled with tears. "But now I think my job was to hold the power for you."

"If I can't be hurt, why did you warn me to be careful of the—"

"I didn't say you couldn't be *hurt*, I meant you couldn't be locked in a witch bottle for all eternity. A bullet between your eyes would take you out just as well," the old woman said with some exasperation. "Look here. You could pass the power even after you're dead, but you'd still be *dead*. And good luck finding a full-fledged witch descended from the coven to pass the power to in *this* town. There ain't one. The chance to break the curse would be *lost*."

I sat in silence, thinking.

My own childhood mystery was paling compared to the machinations at work in Mystic's End. Who my mother was individually was *almost* a secondary question. The first question—who I was—had been answered.

I was this generation's daughter of the first coven of Mystic's End.

"Are you ever going to tell Gabe who you were?" I asked her after a while.

"I wondered when you would finally ask me that question." Miss Bessie smirked as she leaned forward and patted my knee. "You want to know why I hid it from him?"

I nodded.

"Because I knew that once *he* knew, he would never stop looking for his mother's bottle," Miss Bessie told me, her voice soft and absent her usual caustic tone. "I didn't want it to consume him. Especially when I knew I couldn't find it myself. And even if I *could*, I had almost no hope of breaking it and freeing her. I love him too much to see him live with this...helplessness."

"Why haven't you *pushed* me harder?" I blurted out, guilt flooding me. "You're basically telling me I might be able to find your daughter and free her from an eternal prison! I would have...I would have done something! Worked harder, studied more, looked into it—"

"Oh, child." Miss Bessie shook her head. "We come to who we are in our *own* time. I think, maybe, you're taking a step off the train in your own station now. No one can force you to face who you are, Fortuna. Not me, not the *visus*, no one. You know now because it was time. You were ready. *You'll* tell Gabe when it's time. You'll know when he's ready. When you're ready."

I stared at her. *I* have to tell Gabe?

"And you'll *have* to do it before you two get married," Miss Bessie answered my thought, her tone returning to her usual demanding self. "If you hide it until you two have three kids and a house in the hills, Gabe will—"

"Enough." I raised my hand. "Is that some prophecy thing, too? The *marry my grandson* thing?"

"No, dear, I just *like* you," Miss Bessie winked. "And it's time that boy settled down."

* * *

I decided the easiest way to get my friends off the case was just to claim there was no case.

"Yes, I just made a mistake," I told Pepper. "The urn wasn't a replica, after all."

Pepper, Ollie, and Gabe stared at me, their mouths open wide.

"What?" I asked, struggling to keep my tone neutral. "I'm not perfect, you know. Sometimes, I make mistakes. I took another look at the urn when I was over there, and I realized I had made a mistake. That's all. It's real, after all."

"You made a *mistake*," Pepper said slowly, hands on her hips.

"Isn't that what I just said?"

"How could *you* make a *mistake*?"

"Look at the evidence," I told her as I gestured toward the table. "We have video and documentation of where that urn was the whole time. No one exchanged it. No one was videoed near it, or blocking the camera in such a way that they could have made some Indiana Jones-like switcheroo. I'm the only person that said it was a fake, and when I went back to look at it? I realized I was wrong. That's all. Sorry for wasting everyone's time."

Ollie nodded as if my explanation made perfect sense and was no skin off his nose. Pepper looked furious there was no mystery to be solved. Gabe, on the other hand, looked like he knew *something* was off in my explanation, but he just couldn't put his finger on *what* it was.

Even Gideon was looking at me strangely.

"I don't believe you," Pepper said, her voice cynically resentful.

"Just *think* about it," I told her as I picked up the evidence and dumped it all into the trash.

"But what about all the other...ooh, actually, this *wasn't* a complete waste of time," Pepper said as she snatched her notebook off the table before I could dump it in the trash. "We found a vampire!"

"We didn't *find* a vampire," I told her.

"I'm going to interview Jeeves for my blog," Pepper continued, ignoring me and completely forgetting about the case of the stolen urn. Within seconds, she shifted focus completely, hot on the trail of a vampire. "Hey, can you give me a ride over to the Complex?" she asked Ollie. "He's probably trailing Martin around as usual."

"Sure." Ollie nodded as he stood up and headed toward the stairs. "Maybe afterward we can get a drink?" His impish expression made the invitation *seem* casual, but it felt like anything but.

Pepper's eyes widened. Then she nodded. "Um, sure." She nodded again, forcing her face into the most ridiculous nonchalant expression I'd ever seen. "Yeah, I'll probably be thirsty by then. Sure. They have good lemonade there. Yep."

"Whatever you wish, my lady." Ollie bowed deeply. "Your chariot awaits."

Pepper giggled and blushed as Gabe and I glanced at one another, sharing a smile.

* * *

"There," Gabe said as he laid a broom against my wall. "It's a living room again."

"Thanks for your help."

"Any time."

Gabe stood straight, his shoulders back. I noticed that, unlike me, he never really lowered his head much. His stance seemed less about posture than a sense of surety, of security in who he was. Even with all the wild and crazy stuff I seemed to have brought into his life, Gabe Wilcox always seemed to stand tall.

"What is it?" he asked, curious about my intense gaze. Looking down, he examined his shirt. "Did I get something on me, paint, or something?"

I shook my head. "You and your grandmother both just always seem to stand so...proud. I don't know. Like nothing rattles either one of you for very long."

Gabe hesitated for a moment. "I don't know that's *entirely* true. We've had our share of shocks, you know." He smiled at me. "*You've* brought a few of them."

"You still think I'm a hippie gypsy?" I asked, laughing.

"I noticed you stopped wearing those clothes after that night." He frowned. "I felt bad about that."

"You felt *bad* about the fact that I started wearing jeans and t-shirts?"

"I felt guilty that my being judgmental—

unfairly—might have led you to change who you are, how you presented yourself," Gabe admitted. "You were new to town. Not only did I go out of my way to make you feel unwelcome, but I also insulted you."

"You did, a little," I replied. "But I wanted to fit in. You made me realize I might have to work a little at it. That small towns don't accept outsiders like me very easily."

Gabe frowned again. "You still feel like an outsider?"

His question surprised me, though I don't know why it should have. I did, often, talk like an outsider. Despite that, I was feeling like one less and less.

"Not as much anymore," I said. "A little, sometimes. But as time passes, I feel more and more like I belong here. Like I was meant to be here."

"I'm glad." Gabe nodded. "Because I'm sure happy you showed up."

I wondered if Gabe would still be happy once he discovered who I was, who his grandmother had been, and what had happened to his mother. As we stood there staring at one another, I thought about telling him everything—but decided against it.

Before I *touched* one bottle, I needed to buckle down and look into whether what everyone was telling me was true. Discover all I could about the curse, about how Addie found the bottles, and what Martin's parade of witches *really* meant.

I didn't know if they were telling the truth.

I didn't know if the truth Miss Bessie was telling me was correct.

I needed to do what I *should* have been doing all along instead of chasing down someone else's stolen urn—learn to scry like the book told me to. Develop my own understanding of just who these people were, and *what* this curse was.

I needed to stop pretending I wasn't a witch, wrapping myself in psychic cotton like a china doll and tamping down the powers I had been given.

Because it was clear now that only a witch could unravel the mysteries of Mystic's End.

The last full witch of the Delphi Coven.

And for better or worse, *I* was that witch.

* * *

THANK YOU FOR READING!

I hope you enjoyed The Art of Scrying! Please think about leaving a review! Fortuna and Gideon's adventures continue in Book 5, The Greyt Escape!

KEEP UP WITH LEANNE LEEDS

Thanks so much for reading! I hope you liked it! Want to keep up with me?

Visit leanneleeds.com to:

Find all my books...

Sign up for my newsletter...

Like me on Facebook...

Follow me on Twitter...

Follow me on Instagram...

Thanks again for reading!

Leanne Leeds

FIND A TYPO? LET US KNOW!

Typos happen. It's sad, but true.

Though we go over the manuscript multiple times, have editors, have beta readers, and advance readers it's inevitable that determined typos and mistakes sometimes find their way into a published book.

Did you find one? If you did, think about reporting it on leanneleeds.com so we can get it corrected.

www.ingramcontent.com/pod-product-compliance
Lightning Source LLC
Chambersburg PA
CBHW031939240626
47153CB00003B/796